PRETTY MAIDS ALL IN A ROW

•

Michelle Buckman
and
A.H. Jackson

AVALON BOOKS
NEW YORK

Published by Thomas Bouregy & Co., Inc.
160 Madison Avenue, New York, NY 10016

Library of Congress Cataloging-in-Publication Data

Buckman, Michelle.
    Pretty maids all in a row / Michelle Buckman and A.H. Jackson.
        p. cm.
    Novel.
    ISBN 0-8034-9778-4 (alk. paper)
    I. Jackson, A.H. II. Title.

PS3602.U28P74 2006
813'.6—dc22

                                        2005037651

PRINTED IN THE UNITED STATES OF AMERICA
ON ACID-FREE PAPER
BY HADDON CRAFTSMEN, BLOOMSBURG, PENNSYLVANIA

Dedicated to my wife Maria, for infinite patience.—AHJ

To my loving family, the best part of this madcap adventure called life.—MB

Chapter One

"**D**ead nuns!"

J. B. Kale looked up from the embossed invitation in his hand to the mischievous twinkling eyes of his business partner, Tori Roche. The black-haired, barefoot beauty lounged on the corner of his desk, her legs draped casually off the edge.

"Dead nuns?" Kale repeated back to her.

"Murdered, actually, a very long time ago. Funny, I thought everyone knew about the nursery rhyme murders." Tori propped her arm on his computer monitor and nodded toward the invitation that read:

Lord Alexander Bertillon
Requests the Honor of Your Presence at a
Mary Mystery Weekend
The Priory Hotel
Wychwood, Oxfordshire.

"He's had one these parties every week for a month. They've really become quite popular. The party theme is the murders of those twelve nuns of Wychwood—the nursery rhyme murders. You know, "Mary Mary quite contrary, how does your garden grow? With silver bells and cockleshells and pretty maids all in a row." That rhyme is really a clue to one of the most diabolical crimes in English history, one that Lord Bertie is doing his best to solve."

"I thought the nursery rhyme referred to Mary, Queen of Scots."

"Blimey, yes, but somebody started chanting the nursery rhyme in connection with the murder of Mary's girls, and it stuck.

Kale smiled and leaned back in his chair. "You wouldn't be pulling my leg?"

"Gad, but you Americans can be so blank about history. You can't mean you've never heard of the massacre of Mary's girls in 1785? They had their heads cut off, Kale. Then, whoever did the foul deed popped the bodies into a big fruit press and squeezed them dry as cornhusks. Twelve women murdered and no one has ever figured out why. And would you believe Lord Bertie's hotel is the old Priory right across the road from the church where it all happened? I didn't go in the church while I was there; the hotel was creepy enough. Big and riddled with secret passages. Its whole ambience revolves around that mystery. You'll probably like it, Kale. I had lunch there last week while you were in New York."

Kale knew the rhyme, but had never heard its grotesque tie to the murder of twelve women. The mystery didn't surprise him, though. He hadn't been in England long—he had worked in London a little more than two years and had rarely been out of the city—but the entire country proved to be steeped in mystery.

He eyed Tori. Old murders didn't interest him nearly as much as knowing the identity of her lunch date. He guessed the lucky fellow was retired CID inspector Harry Bass. Kale liked the man well enough; in fact he owed his career to the man, but would have liked him better at a distance—far away from Tori.

Kale leaned back wishing he had eyes as dark as Tori's, but with bushy eyebrows to make him look imposing. His baby blues were as docile as a child's. "Harry took you to lunch, I suppose?"

"Go on. Of course Harry took me. It was his idea. Anyway, as I was saying, those poor nuns were beheaded and all their blood squeezed out in the cellar of that church; in a fruit press, like oranges."

"Squeezed? Why would anyone do that?"

"Bertie thinks they were looking for something and attempting to make Mary Gant talk. A treasure of some sort, which he doesn't think they ever found. He's fascinated by it all and absolutely bent on solving the crime."

Kale didn't want to think about crime, old or new. Tori flooded his senses. She had on the reddest lipstick today. And her hair, hanging in soft waves to her shoulders, was dark and shiny; he wished he could run his fingers through it. Too bad she was attracted to older, financially secure men like Harry. And now it seemed Lord Bertillon was another suitor begging for her attention. "Who's Bertie?"

Tori laughed. Kale wore his thoughts on his face. "I only met him last week. He's a darling man, but not my sort. Besides, he's totally engrossed in solving that mystery. He didn't even notice me. In fact, I felt rather green and prickly with Harry and him being such fast pals."

When she leaned forward, one hand planted on the desk, Kale made a point of looking at her face and not her perfect figure.

She took a deep breath and continued. "The hotel's restaurant is fascinating, Kale. Big, and hardly changed since the old days. And the fare is excellent. I had "Mary's Soup" for starters; a cold raspberry soup with thirteen croutons. Everytime I ate one, Bertie would name one of the murdered nuns, just to tease me. He called them Mary's girls. They never found the heads, or any trace of Prioress Mary Gant. Legend has her having participated in the crime and running away with something valuable."

"Like what?"

"I'm not sure even Bertie knows. If he does, he's not telling."

The intrigue made Tori look even more radiant than usual. Kale pulled his eyes away from her and fixed his gaze instead at the photo on the corner of his desk, trying to concentrate on the story, but the faces staring back at him from the photo only distracted him further. The photo was two years old, taken the week before he left the States. His family remained frozen in his mind at that instant. His sister, ponytailed and bright-faced, looked like a kid but no longer sounded like one on the telephone. She was seventeen now. His mother's laughing brown eyes streamed with tears over his leaving. His father stood ramrod-straight glaring at him, a look that kept Kale honest down to the smallest business detail. Some days he missed them terribly, but today the picture couldn't take his mind off Tori. Her presence overwhelmed him and made him feel like a schoolboy. It was a wonder they'd managed to write a dozen books side by side. He could barely keep up his end of a conversation without getting lost in her exotic perfume.

He chewed the end of his pencil. "This Prioress Mary Gant was something other than a nun?"

Tori bent one leg and looked at him suggestively. "Mary was a very astute businesswoman."

It took Kale half a second to comprehend her meaning. "She was a hooker?"

"Not at all. She was an entertainer and entrepreneur. At the time of the murders she was supplying every tavern in Britain with fruit brandy. And she did it all under the nose of the king's tax collector."

"A bootlegger . . . and since they never found her body, quite possibly a mass murderer? She chose a very unlikely alias." Kale couldn't help laughing. "You laugh, but that was the middle of the eighteenth century and times were hard. Prioress Mary Gant was a woman's woman. Don't sell her short."

Tori's face flushed across high cheekbones. The mystery of the murders excited her, obviously, but there was something more. One thing he'd learned about his Brit partner over the last two years was how much she loved parties. Tori had a constant string of events to attend: cocktail parties, costume parties, gallery openings, wine and cheese gatherings, book signings and poetry readings. He accompanied her on occasion, when she chose to include him, especially the more literary gatherings of writers and poets. Kale figured it was the anticipation of an upcoming weekend-long party that had her keyed up.

He thought over the invitation a little more seriously. An entire weekend ensconced with Tori in a medieval inn. This party, away from the pressures of the office, might be the perfect opportunity to deepen their relationship, to let her know how he really felt.

He fingered the invitation, formally addressed to them both: *Victoria Anne Roche & Joseph Bently Kale, of Galley Press.*

"Who told this Lord Bertie my full name?"

Kale detested his Christian name. "Joe," after his father, as if he wasn't worth one of his own. "Bently" didn't even bear thinking about. He never answered to or signed anything beyond "Kale." Then it dawned on him. "Harry!"

"I thought that would get a rise." Tori stood, smoothed a crease from her red leather skirt and crossed the room to pick up a pair of sling-backs with two-inch heels. "Anyway," she said, buckling her left sandal, "that's the party theme: the nursery rhyme murders."

"Those murders happened over two hundred and fifty years ago. Why are Harry Bass and this Lord Bertie character—and for that matter, you—so interested?"

She rolled her eyes. "Bertie is using it to draw

tourists. He's hoping the parties will garner some publicity and put Wychwood on the tour maps. I don't know why Harry should be so interested. He stumbled onto Bertie's place about a month ago—you know, when he went looking for that new mare for his stable. Maybe after hearing Bertie's rendition of the crime, his policeman's ego couldn't stand the suspense of not knowing the truth. Personally, I intend to turn the whole murder ordeal into a novel and make us some money. I want to see my name on a cover for once, instead of doing all this ghostwriting. Come to think of it, maybe that's what Harry wants too, another Harry book."

Harry had been forced into early retirement from the Criminal Investigation Department of the London police and responded by pilfering his best case-files, which he duly sold to Kale's boss, the famed publisher, Enoch Tulley. Tori and the newly hired Kale had written the files into the hugely successful, fast-paced mysteries dubbed "the Harry Books."

Another book deal wouldn't be enough to press Harry into attending a party. Kale suspected there was more to the story than Tori was letting on, but he held his thoughts in check. Her reasons were valid enough; Galley Press had been in the red from the word *go* and Kale agreed that neither he nor Tori had been given the recognition they deserved on the Harry Books. The entire series had been released under Harry's name; as ghostwriters, Victoria Roche and J. B. Kale didn't get any of credit.

Tori finished buckling her other shoe before turning to face him. "In the year since Mr. Tulley crashed his car and we inherited this establishment, all we've put on the lists are cookbooks. We need a best-seller, and quickly."

"Not our fault Tulley died without having paid taxes for ten years."

"No, but we shouldn't have agreed to sign over all the Harry Books to Inland Revenue. We caved in like undercooked soufflés."

We caved in on all but this last book, Kale acknowledged silently to himself. And he'd had threats about it he hadn't mentioned to Tori. Or at least he surmised it was the Harry Book the blackmailer was after. *If you value your business, you'll give up the goods,* the fax had read the previous Monday, followed by the same message for four consecutive days. He didn't think Tori was up to handling more stress than they were already suffering financially, so he'd kept mum, waiting to see if anything more would come of it. Nothing had. His only thought was someone wanted the incriminating evidence Harry had given them for the plot of the last book, but that seemed hard to believe. Kale tried to put it from his mind. Surely nothing would come of it. They had to be empty threats. "Harry thought it wise to give the whole lot of them over to the taxes. We held out this last one, though. Don't forget it."

"Need I remind you, while he's raising horses in Ireland, we are near to bankruptcy. That one title isn't going to save us. Harry's readership is down and we're not likely to sell out the first printing. We are going to solve the nursery rhyme murders and write a best-seller."

She strode out the door, but paused in the hallway.

"Oh, I forgot, Harry called to say he'd be in today. Ta!" With a clatter of heels on terrazzo, she fled down the office stairs and headed for the front door.

Kale moved to the window and watched Tori slow traffic on Bayswater Road. He was so absorbed he failed to notice Neddy Linquist enter with lunch.

"Ham and cheese all right?" asked the secretary.

Kale jumped and turned around. One inch short of five feet, with a hair bun jammed through with pencils, Neddy smiled and plunked down a sandwich along with a heavy block of paper. Kale lifted off the sandwich, dusted the crumbs from the stack of printed pages and read the title. "Ah, not another cookbook!"

Neddy shrugged, "Any port in a financial storm."

Mr. Enoch Tulley had built Galley Press into a sizable publishing house with a reputation for a wide variety of quality books, and now they were down to only publishing cookbooks.

Kale and Tori's inheritance of Galley Press had come as a huge surprise, but without the *Harry Books* all they really had were forty stale titles suited only for the Christmas book market, and a mortgaged two-story Serge Chermayoff–designed office building on Bayswater Road across from Hyde Park. They were lucky that Tulley's secretary and bookkeeper, Neddy Linquist, had stayed on with them. Fully apprised of all things, including company finances, the woman had kept them afloat by sheer willpower . . . and cookbooks.

Kale sat and tapped the manuscript with a pencil. "Neddy, after this one, I have no idea what we're going to publish. If we don't find something quickly I may have to head for home. I can't even pay my next month's rent." Home meant back to the States, back to Riverside, Michigan, a small town he'd never left until college. He'd finally escaped it, and then the entire country when a professor mentioned a friend of his in London needed an editor. Kale had accepted without hesitation, a choice he had never regretted.

He didn't want to give up now. He was finally his own boss in the book industry, a dream come true. All he lacked were his own books. He'd carried ideas around in his head for years, waiting to pour them down on paper, but he'd grown so much as a writer he couldn't work with his old stories. He needed something new and unique for the Press. He had to quit editing cookbooks and find something he could put to paper himself.

Neddy smiled in her efficient, no-nonsense way. "You'll think of something, Kale. You can't go home. You have unfinished business here." She plucked three chewed pencils from his cluttered desk and deposited three newly sharpened ones in his catchall. "Our most meaningful stories come from looking to the past and applying insights from the present. Great stories endure. That's where your story is, in the enduring past."

Kale could rarely decipher Neddyisms. He waited until she retreated out of his office before taking a bite of the sandwich. "Ah, American mustard." Neddy always remembered the mustard. Smart woman. He relished every mouthful as he pondered her words of wisdom: *Look to the enduring past.* Certainly not his. He'd had a perfectly happy childhood, fishing and playing with his dog on a riverbank, with an equally boring teen life, all of which equaled absolutely nothing to write about.

He reached for the party invitation. Prioress Mary Gant's past? Now there, just maybe, was an enduring tale. And it might take his mind off the threat against the business.

Thinking of Tori's optimism, he signed the RSVP and tossed it into his out-box.

Chapter Two

Friday afternoon they were on their way to the Priory Hotel in Harry's car.

Kale sat in the back of the big Mercedes, one arm flung across the back of the seat, his long legs cramping. He shifted into the corner with some difficulty and crossed one leg over the other.

He should have driven his own car, an older model Jaguar with lots of power, miles, and dents, but Tori had said she liked Harry's best, which would figure. She had a longing for luxury and was determined to end up with a life better than the one she'd left behind in Manchester, where she'd been crowded in with her five sisters with nothing to claim as her own. He knew it wasn't greed motivating her, rather a resolute promise to rise above the abject poverty that had claimed her siblings. Two of them had become pregnant and gotten married before completing school, which easily justified why Tori flirted outrageously without committing to anyone. She readily admitted her intention to fall in love selectively or else not at all. Kale couldn't imagine her choosing Harry. Nevertheless, he'd decided it was better to ride along with them in Harry's car than worry about what transpired in his absence.

Harry drove like an old fart, a manner that belied his forty-six years. Tori turned sideways in the front seat, jangled her bracelets, and talked without waiting for replies.

Kale watched half-amused, half-irritated, as Tori carefully split her attention between them and the passing countryside. Harry was too old for a girl like Tori, but she didn't see it that way. He held more secrets in his balding head than the Holy Grail, and mystery enthralled her. Of course, Harry's tough alley-brawler image and cool exterior helped. So did his wide shoulders and thick arms.

Kale reflected on his own image—six-foot-two, blond hair, and blue eyes. A typical American beach boy with khakis and tailored polo shirts bought as close to Saville Row as his limited income would allow. He went out of his way to dress well. Harry always dressed like what he was, a cop—brown suit, brown shoes, and a blue oxford shirt.

Kale shifted his legs and sighed; since he'd finished proofing the cookbook galleys on Thursday, they'd all decided to leave early for the mystery weekend to celebrate. The edits were done. Work was over. In fact, if this weekend didn't inspire a book, all of Galley Press' work was over. It was publish or perish time. A failure at this juncture would mean back to the States and back to teaching. There wouldn't be much pride in that. He and Tori had to come up with a new book venture, and fast. Maybe Tori would follow through on this mystery about dead nuns, but he didn't see it happening. Time had closed that case permanently. He laid his head back on the seat, listening to the rise and fall of her voice as she discussed the party.

"My costume is so real, you won't believe it's me. Oh, no, I'm not telling what it is."

Kale couldn't imagine anything disguising Tori that completely. He would know her anywhere.

Tori glanced over the seat, "I can't wait to see what costume Bertie gives you, Kale."

"I'm weak from anticipation," he replied. He hadn't thought of having to wear a costume. He hadn't really thought much about the party at all. The history surrounding the nursery rhyme murders interested him more and more, but he thought celebrating it was frivolous. He had a business to run, one on the brink of failure.

Harry met his eyes in the rearview mirror; his reflection bore a thinly disguised smirk. He could be a weasel at times, too slick and sneaky for somebody built like a tractor. Too bad the guy was so likable. "Relax, Kale, it should be fun. And who knows, you might solve the puzzle and make yourself famous. But I want you both to be very careful."

Tori glanced from Harry to Kale, and back. "What exactly is that supposed to mean, Harry?"

Kale kept his eyes trained on the mirror, waiting for the explanation.

Harry remained tight-lipped until he stopped at the next intersection, then he half-turned in his seat and wagged a stubby finger. "This goes no further, understood?"

Kale nodded. Looking puzzled, Tori reacted with a tilt of her head and a raised eyebrow.

"The file has never been closed on the nursery rhyme murders. The police have always known who did it; only they could never come up with any proof. They're still trying."

"Wait a sec," Kale said. "Why would the police waste time on such an old case?"

"Well they're not, are they? They're wasting ours."

The trio went silent for a moment. Kale tried not to imagine the murder scene, but couldn't cast it aside. It throbbed there with the nagging wonder of what hadn't been solved after two hundred and fifty years. "Harry, what was there to kill for? Is this some kind of weird hunt for a motive? The case is ancient. Life goes on, everything has changed."

Harry glared into the mirror. "Nothing has changed." Then he faced front, punched down on the gas pedal and kept his eyes glued to the road.

"So, what's the deal, Harry? Who did the dastardly deed? And why?"

Harry shrugged, and drove a bit faster.

A river sparkled alongside the road then passed under the car as they traversed a stone bridge. Kale gave up on Harry and laid his head back. Turning his head to face the window, he gazed out at the lush green of the Wychwood Forest. Who would have figured a whole forest of oak trees? "Don't they ever cut them down? Those things are huge."

Tori turned and smacked his arm. "Here we are! Wychwood Village."

Kale had never seen such a forlorn-looking main street. No light standards, no kids playing, no dogs barking, and no window glass in any of the stone houses. "It's a ghost town."

"There's the old church," Tori said, pointing.

Kale cast a writer's gaze toward the structure, the infamous site of the nursery rhyme murders. Behind a low stone wall, the surprisingly well-preserved gray stone building stood some forty feet back from the road with a broken brick walkway leading up to a mammoth door hung on large black hinges. The slate roof looked to be in poor repair, missing patches of shingles. Weeds covered the grounds around the building and competed with knee-high grass turning golden in the summer sun. It was easy to imagine how spooky the place would look at night.

The old mystery of missing heads, motive, and blood could wait. Kale ached to stretch his legs. At the end of a wide expanse of well-kept lawn, the hotel rose before them, gray stone and narrow windows, like an elderly sentinel overlooking the chapel across the way.

Leaving Harry to carry in the luggage, Tori and Kale strolled up the wide flagstone steps to the dim innards of the hotel lobby, lit only by the pale glow of mock gas lanterns. Kale passed their company charge card across the worn mahogany reception desk. "Galley Press. Victoria Roche, J. B. Kale, and Harry Bass. We're here for the party weekend."

The receptionist, a pinched-faced brunet looking like part of the scenery in an eighteenth-century style, full-length brown woolen dress, took his card and shook her head. "I'm so sorry about your building. We just saw it on the telly." She pointed behind to the one modern convenience in a sea of antiques.

Kale stared at the TV, but saw only the end of a weather report. "Pardon me? You're sorry about what?"

"Oh my, you haven't heard. I can't imagine I'm the first to tell you. Your office building, across from Hyde Park, it burned down. Lord Bertillon was here watching. He said it was your building."

Tori bit her knuckles. "Neddy! Oh my, she simply has to be all right."

Kale stared dumbfounded at the receptionist. *The threat. The blackmailer had ruined his business. What did he want? What would he do next?*

Tori pulled on Harry's sleeve as he arrived at her side catching the tail end of the news. "Harry, we must go back and find Neddy."

Kale held her in place as he spoke to the receptionist. "Did the news mention any casualties? Did they say what caused the fire?"

"I'm afraid they didn't mention a cause, sir. But they did say no one was injured."

Both Kale and Tori breathed audible sighs of relief, while from behind Harry said, "I should have antici-pated something like this."

Tori turned and looked at him, shocked, "Anticipate our business would burn down? Are you crazy?"

Kale looked from one to the other, disbelieving. Was he implying arson? How could Harry have known about the threat? Was someone really out to ruin them? Or, perhaps even silence them over a story file? It made no sense.

"Insurance . . ." said Harry slowly, "do you have adequate insurance?"

"Don't be silly. Of course we do. Neddy wouldn't let a day go by that wasn't fully insured," Tori said, exasperated. She flipped out her cell phone and dialed, but no one answered at Neddy's apartment.

Kale tried to roughly calculate their policies in his head: inventory, loss of business, policy deductions, and returns. He figured they'd come out even, if not slightly ahead, at least enough to invest in new office equipment. But Neddy was his only real concern. There wasn't much need to rush back to a pile of rubble. He couldn't stand the idea of getting back in Harry's car again without good cause. "I've got Neddy's cell phone number. I'll call from the room. We'll decide what to do after speaking with her."

"Well ducks," Harry said, "seems to me you should be doing handstands to be rid of that bloody awful building."

Tori glowered at him. "I loved that building. But you're right about those old remainders. We hadn't a hope of selling them. Maybe we'll get the costs back."

"Harry," Kale began, "if this has anything to do with this weekend, I'll—"

His intention was cut short. A slight man with a gone-to-seed mustache entered the room. Tori pushed between Harry and Kale to meet him.

"Bertie! My lovely building is gone," she exclaimed as she ran forward to be swept up in sympathetic, noble arms.

The Lord's pleated pants looked like something held over from the sixties. He wore a vest without a suit jacket and a gold watch chain draped from a buttonhole into a pocket. Lord Alexander Bertillon, owner of the Priory. The man who relished ancient murder mysteries.

Lord Bertillon, his right arm wrapped around Tori's waist, stepped up, snatched the Galley Press charge card from the receptionist, and handed it back to Kale. "Victoria's friends are my friends and will have the upper suite, compliments of the establishment."

Kale liked him immediately; he appeared to have a reckless charm not unlike Tori's, as if the two were kindred spirits. The receptionist nodded, and smiled gravely. "I've told them about the fire."

"Most unfortunate. If there's anything I can do, please don't hesitate to ask. In the meantime, let's get you to your suites." He led them past the curving front staircase of the reception area and down a hallway toward the sound of raised voices, pot lids being jostled, and a knife steadily chopping against a block.

"The kitchen," Bertie said, pointing as he skirted around a pile of linens and headed up a narrow, dimly lit flight of stairs. Tori clipped along in her heels, and Harry followed, leaving Kale once again feeling like he was two steps behind.

The staircase was steep and narrow. Their shadows moved strangely over the walls. Odd sounds echoed. Even their footfalls and labored breathing became magnified as they progressed upward, step by step. At the twist of the first flight Kale spotted the outline of a door. He paused, curious, and tempted to find the catch that opened it, but the sound of Tori's throaty laughter stopped him, and he hurried to catch up. On the next landing, he felt the edge of the wall, expecting another hidden door, but couldn't find the outline. He rushed to catch up and saw his companions disappear, one after the other, through a doorway. Kale followed into a small grubby room with a book-strewn table and a dilapidated, overstuffed gold velvet chair occupied by a sleeping Persian cat. Bertie fiddled with a bookshelf, which after a moment pulled away from the wall to become a desk. Bertie winked at Tori, while Harry stepped in behind, leaving Kale with the purring cat.

Kale advanced on the desk. Papers were spread about, obviously in some sort of organized manner, but completely meaningless to him until Harry picked up a dog-eared manuscript from the nearest pile and threw it to Kale.

The author's name was blacked out, but he read the title aloud, "*History of the Mad Monks of Mendelenham.* They make that awful green liqueur my mother buys at Christmas."

"Right you are, Christmas Green. What would the holiday be without a bottle of the green? They make jam, marmalade, and other fruit spirits as well. But I wouldn't bother reading that manuscript; it's just an outline of self-promotion supplied by the monks to your old boss, Enoch Tulley. All invented rubbish! No help with the puzzle." Bertie's eyes danced with excitement.

Kale scratched his head. Tulley? What did Enoch Tulley have to do with Bertie's mystery other than the fact he'd attended one of the parties? "Tulley was putting together a book for them?"

"Certainly," Tori replied. "A history of the area. That's why he came up here."

Kale blinked. Tulley doing a history book? No doubt it would have included recipes. Tulley had a thing for cookbooks. He claimed they would sell when nothing else would.

Kale shook the thoughts away. How had he remained clueless to so much going on around him? He couldn't even figure out what part of Bertie's mystery the party guests were meant to solve. Were they meant to figure out where the Mary's girls' heads were buried? Or maybe why they were killed? "Lord Bertillon, I don't understand what—"

Bertie held up a hand. "None of that 'Lord' stuff with me, lad. Bertie will do nicely, thank you. And how rude of me to forget how far you have traveled." The sprightly Lord walked over and pushed a panel on the far side of the room. It slid open noiselessly. Bertie turned and motioned them down another narrow, twisting passage. Kale decided the passage ran between the guestrooms and he wondered how many had secret panels. "Like a honeycomb," he muttered.

At last, Bertie stopped. "This is the one." He raised his hand and groped around a section of wall. A breath later, a door swung open into a magnificent fireplace as tall as the innkeeper himself. "We could have come up the front steps, of course, but then you wouldn't have known how to find the kitchen in the middle of the night." He laughed, and Kale grimaced, knowing he could never find his way back to the kitchen through that maze.

Kale ducked his head, stepped through the entrance and whistled at the guest suite's grand proportions. The fireplace he'd stepped through was part of a sitting area flanked by a wall of leaded glass windows. But the muted velvets and finery of the furnishings were suddenly lost on Kale as his full attention went to the wall behind the ivory satin duvet-covered bed, to the life-size portrait of a woman dressed in black.

Kale swallowed and looked at Tori, who stood watching his reaction with humorous expectations. There was no doubt about the connection. The woman in the painting was a dead ringer.

"Close your mouth, Kale, and say hello to my many-times great grandmother, the Prioress Mary Gant."

Chapter Three

Kale was shown to a small bedroom adjoining Tori's grand suite. She hadn't elaborated much on her relationship to Mary Gant. She said it would keep till the evening, and he was a patient man. Bertie had left them to wash up and relax before the noon meal. Kale's bathroom fit the English vernacular to a tee. "A loo and behold, no shower," he yelled. He decided he and Tori were meant to share the larger bathroom. For the time being, he made do with the small sink.

"Kale," Tori yelled from the next room, "Harry spied that portrait while doing a bit of sleuthing for Bertie. That's why I was here while you were in New York."

Relieved, Kale ran some water in the basin and jumped when the pipes rumbled. Laughing at his timidity, he splashed his face and frowned at his reflection in the blurred antique mirror. There were too many worries hung on it with the building burned down, insurance claims to contend with, no new books on the horizon, two mysteries to solve . . . and the fight for Tori's affections. He'd intended to set things clear with her all along, but not until the business was fixed and profitable. Now it looked like that would never be.

"Your family name used to be Gant?" he hollered back.

"That's right. It was changed a long time ago, for rather obvious reasons." Tori rapped lightly on his door. "Might I come in?"

"Sure, if you want to see me naked."

"Sounds inviting. But it might put me off lunch. I'm starved. Have you heard from Neddy? I'm so worried, Kale."

"No, not yet. But she'll be all right. Nothing can harm our Neddy. She's made of hard stuff. You go down to lunch. I'll stay here until I get her on the phone."

Neddy phoned in before he had a chance to call her. She was fine. "Sorry I was so long getting in touch, but I've been busy with the insurance man. It's gone, Kale, the whole shebang. It's just a pile of ashes. But hang on to your hat, young man, there is a bright side." She quoted a proposed settlement figure that put a spark in his eye. "And that's not all, you have an offer for the property." She laughed, and quoted a sum so large that Kale had to ask her to repeat it while he searched out a chair.

"Is it a definite offer? I mean, is there real money?"

"Well, of course there's money. I have a check right here on my desk. That's the lovely thing about owning prime real estate. The lucky prospective buyer happened to catch the newscast on the telly and rang up his agent. It's not enough to pay up all the back taxes, but it's enough to give us a good start to get going again. Maybe not in downtown London, but somewhere close." Neddy told him she had already taken care of most of the paperwork, leaving little for them to do other than sign the papers. "That can wait. You two carry on with your weekend. There's nothing to be done except sift through the ash and rubble and I've hired some people for that. Oh, almost forgot. The insurance man told me the fire started in the cleaning cupboard. He thought the cause was a short in the alarm system. They found a control box or something, and it recorded the cause of the short: Somebody broke into our office."

Kale, having very briefly entertained thoughts that Neddy had torched the place, sounded relieved. "Neddy, we don't have an alarm system."

"That's what I told him. But then I remembered the wall safe—the one in your office. It had a very expensive alarm that was never turned off."

"We couldn't turn it off. Mr. Tulley took the combination to his grave. You said there was nothing in that safe."

"The coppers got it open; at least that's what the insurance man told me. But he didn't know if they found anything. I can't imagine there was anything in there. Tulley never owned anything of value except the Press."

In spite of Neddy's assurance, a sense of urgency

welled up in him for a moment. He needed to see the remnants of their building with his own eyes, to see if anything was salvageable. Then he shoved the idea aside. He'd have to rely on Neddy to trudge through the wreckage and look for anything of value. And Harry was probably right about it being safer away from the place. Certainly no one was more capable of handling the crisis than Neddy. There was nothing to be accomplished from rushing back to the wreckage.

Saying good-bye, he walked over to his suitcase and retrieved suitable hotel lunch attire—a crisp white shirt and charcoal trousers. He grabbed a maroon-colored tie, and, walking into the bathroom thinking of the quirky Lord Bertillon, wondered what game the man was playing. He slid the knot up his tie with a bit too much force. "Lunch," he said, "then we'll see where things go from there."

Harry's door across the hall was closed and unresponsive to his knock. He shrugged and headed dejectedly toward the main staircase, his steps muffled by the thick gold-colored carpet. He paused at the top step, leaned over the banister, and looked down four stories to the reception area below. There was no one about except the duty hostess. The place looked deserted.

"This way, Mr. Kale. Your friends are waiting on the patio," the hostess said, and led him through an empty dining room to a brick patio adorned with fancy wrought-iron tables and chairs. Huge clay pots of red geraniums stood in the corners, and boxwoods, squared off like a brick wall, bordered the patio on all sides except where a path stepped off into a garden run riot with roses.

Kale stopped, amazed. "Look at them all! It's like a flower shop."

His spinsterish escort paused and mentioned that the bushes were hundreds of years old. "That very large white one in the center was planted by Edward the Confessor. It's called the Confessor Rose. Would you like to walk among them Mr. Kale? I could wait. Shall I tell Lord Bertillon you'll be few minutes?"

"You're very kind, but I think I'd better join my friends."

Kale kept looking back. The smell was almost overwhelming, like an overdose of his mother's perfume. He gazed across the garden, beyond the roses, past the bird feeders, baths, and pole-top birdhouses, to an old vine-covered gardening shed, its wood blackened with age. A cockeyed door and tiny window encrusted with dirt made Kale wonder if the gardener even used it anymore.

The hostess led him to the east-most end of the patio where the branches of an ancient oak tree hung obtrusively into one corner. Seated under its shade, Tori and Harry were chatting congenially with Bertie. A bottle of wine sat chilling.

"Here you are, Mr. Kale. Hope you enjoy your stay," the receptionist said.

"Thank you, Miss . . ."

"Jenkins, sir," she said and smiled in a way that reminded Kale of his kid sister. She turned and walked off in the direction of the dining room.

Tori turned and held her glass toward him. "Cheers, partner. What took you so long?"

Kale's appraisal took in the whole of her. She'd pulled her hair up into some kind of fancy arrangement on the back of her head with wisps hanging loose around her face. Certainly he'd seen her hair up before, but here, in this setting, sipping wine with the oddly debonair Lord Bertillon, she evoked a sense of grace and timelessness he hadn't seen in her before. Perhaps Mary Gant's portrait had changed his perception. Tori's cocky smile now seemed more mysterious. Her ever-perfect posture now seemed more reminiscent of cultured ladies in drawing rooms than merely an appealing trait of his ever-modern associate.

"Sorry. I've been touring a bit," he fibbed as he accepted a proffered glass of claret from Bertie, who he noticed had added a double-breasted dark blue jacket to his attire. Harry's suit remained unchanged—brown. Kale wondered whether the ex-cop's suitcase contained five identical blue shirts, or if he never changed at all. "The place seems rather quiet, Lord Bertillon," Kale said, enjoying the sound of the title. It made him feel a part of the surroundings.

"Bertie. Call me Bertie." He waved Kale into the chair between Harry and Tori. "The hotel is empty for the day, but there'll be visitors aplenty tomorrow." At Bertie's signal, a lingering waitress disappeared, returning moments later to serve them cold poached salmon and asparagus tips arranged on glossy black plates.

Kale flipped his napkin across his lap and delved into the flaky salmon steak. "Neddy called," he said to Tori. "The building is definitely gone, but Neddy is fine and says she's handling things." He quoted the figure Neddy had mentioned over the phone. Tori looked a bit crestfallen. "And we already have an offer for the land," Kale continued. "All told, it's enough to put off a measure of the taxes long enough for a second go-round." He watched her brighten like an opening rose.

"Bloody shame about your building. But accidents do happen," Bertie said.

"Hardly that," Harry muttered through a mouthful of salmon.

Kale cast Bertie an appreciative nod, then stared back at Harry. "Twice now you've insinuated the fire wasn't an accident. Neddy told me the fire started in the alarm box. What do you know, Harry?"

Harry looked him straight in the eye, "I called London and was read the police report. Somebody broke in, and, unable to open that safe in your office, burned the whole place to the ground."

Kale looked dubious. What could Enoch Tulley have had in that safe? "What kind of idiot would burn down our business?"

Bertie twiddled the end of his salmon flaked handlebar mustache. "Harry, I believe you're onto something. What is it you're not telling us?"

Kale sipped tentatively at the sparkling glass of claret. "They didn't have to burn down our building. We would have given them whatever they were looking for."

Harry took a dinner roll from a basket on the table. "I guess *they* had no one to inform them of that small detail."

Tori gazed glassy-eyed into the trees. "I'm now of a mind that the whole thing is a blessing. I'll miss the office, such a beautiful building, but now all those old titles are gone. I'm hoping we find Mary Gant's mysterious treasure somewhere in the inn. We'll be rich *and* I'll have a great mystery to write up. Are all of tomorrow's party guests invited to join the hunt?"

"Righto! Not just a party this go-round, but a treasure hunt. Meanwhile, when you next contact this Neddy person, have her pack up your belongings and forward them to the manor. With your business gone, there's nothing to keep you in the city, and living here you can devote all your time to solving the nursery rhyme murders. No argument now."

Tori fairly jumped at the suggestion. "What a good idea. Thank you, Bertie."

This place is like quicksand; the more we move, the deeper in we get, Kale thought. Then a movement in the garden diverted Kale's attention. Was the shed door propped that far open before? He watched it a moment, expecting a face to appear. "Bertie, you did say we're alone here for the day, didn't you?"

"Most certainly. Only the staff bustling around with last minute details. Are you considering a walk in my garden, Kale?"

"No. Just curious about the old shed."

"I say. Nothing but tools back there. The old thing adds a bit of fright to the scene though, doesn't it? And if you see Potter the gardener, he'll add a shiver to your spine." Bertie chuckled at his own levity.

Kale continued to stare at the shed as he sipped the last of his wine, his unease not put to rest.

"Well," Bertie said, setting his napkin over his plate, "let's be off on our shilling tour of the village."

A few minutes later, the four arranged themselves into the diminutive Lord's dilapidated Bentley limousine. Harry claimed the front seat with Bertie. Kale opened the rear door. "Ladies first." Given the car and the setting, she accepted Kale's gentlemanly offer with a haughty smile and not her usual biting comment about being able to fend for herself.

Kale thought the inside of the car smelled like old shoes.

According to Bertie, Wychwood Village had been built in the loop of the Evenlode River, part of an old canal system, which at one time reached all the way to London. "My family has been here for more than three hundred and fifty years," Bertie said as they drove past a huge ancient timber structure, most likely a warehouse in its day. "At one time," Bertie continued, "Wychwood bustled with life and produced great quantities of lumber, barrels, and quarry slate—slate being the most important."

Kale could easily believe that. All of the twenty or so abandoned houses fronting the high street were constructed of the same gray stone. Even the quarter mile of road between the two identical bridges that defined the village were walled with four feet of the stuff. Kale turned and looked through the back window. "Do you own all those houses, Bertie?"

"Unfortunately, yes. And bloody great nuisances they are too. If I had the funds to put in essential services I'd sell every one and be rid of them."

Tori turned and put her face in the window next to Kale's. I would buy one in a minute," she said. This village is idyllic, Bertie. You could charge anything and people would pay."

"Alas, I'm borrowed out. The hotel has drained me of every cent. A shame really. This village should be bustling with people like it was years ago. The prosperity ended when my family backed the wrong side in the seventeenth-century parliamentary rebellions. For punishment, Cromwell stretched a few of my ancestors' necks and ordered the forest off limits. That effectively put an end to the family fortune. How my esteemed relatives managed is a mystery. I certainly can't. Manor upkeep is considerable, I can assure you."

Tori, her legs almost meeting Kale's in the spacious backseat, perked up, "But when Mary arrived, things must have changed. She brought jobs and prosperity, didn't she?"

Kale wanted to hold her hand. Her childlike interest made him feel protective.

Bertie nodded in answer to Tori. "Right you are, Victoria. Your esteemed relative arrived on the scene two decades after the Cromwell edict. She was a stranger and a mystery to the village, but welcome enough since she did bring a slight revival of fortunes with her wine and jellies, and later with the spirits. But, after her unfortunate demise, prosperity once again withered on the vine." Bertie glanced over his shoulder. "Not to worry, my dear. The Prioress will revive this town yet again. Just you wait and see. I've a great turnout expected for the Mary Mystery weekend. If all goes well, the Priory and the village will be on the tourist maps for sure. Especially with the added attraction of the treasure hunt."

He turned back to the road, pressing the old Bentley hard. It rumbled over a bump, backfired, and continued on. "And," shouted Bertie, "if the party exceeds expectations, we'll have our hands on more money than the tourists will ever bring."

Harry flashed him a grin and gripped the dash as they bounced over a pothole.

Kale turned from the back window and caught Harry's expression. Was he implying there really was treasure to be found? Before he could ask, Harry sat up straight and pointed out the window. "We're back. Let's use my Mercedes next round, shall we? I'm bruised all over."

Tori laughed. "Not posh enough, Harry? You're the only ex-bobby I know who drives a Mercedes."

Just then, a white delivery truck raced out from behind the church and barreled nonstop out the driveway, nearly careening into the Bentley. Kale caught a fleeting glimpse of a thick-necked monster of a man with a head like a buffalo and shoulders to match. Huge baboonlike hands, hairy and thick, grasped the steering wheel.

Kale snatched Tori's hand, but she pulled it free and gasped. "What kind of fool was that?"

Bertie swore, "That was Hermes Wheems. A halfwit if ever there was one."

Kale craned his neck to follow the view of the lorry out the back window. The crazy man jerked the truck haphazardly around a pothole. The lettering on the truck read *Bourton Builders.*

"Hey," cried Tori, "he's from Bourton. Those mad monks of Mendelenham have their abbey in Bourton.

Bertie cleared his throat. "Yes, he works for the Mendelenham monks. They have a factory there. Their abbot, who they call Leviticus, is a bit of an ugly duck. But you can judge that for yourselves; his picture is on your morning marmalade jar." Bertie laughed. "They do make good jam."

"What is that fellow Wheems doing here?" Kale asked.

"He's doing repairs on Mary's church. Good roof man. He fixed the hotel roof, and did a splendid job. The monks are selling Mary's church. If I had the funds, I would buy it. A fruitless ambition, since someone's beat me to an offer. A man named Abner Snow. A London chap. Runs gaming houses or something unsavory. Perhaps you know him?"

"We know Abner Snow, don't we Harrykins?" Tori said, teasing.

Kale knew Tori wouldn't push her teasing too far; Harry was very touchy on the subject of Abner Snow. The man had been a canker in Harry's life for a long time. Tori had told Kale the story ages ago. The first time she met Harry was during her college days, at one of Abner Snow's club openings. She rather liked Abner. Tall, always impeccably dressed, and with a hair color that matched his last name perfectly. Over Harry and

Tori's first drink that night in Oxford, Harry had freely given her his reasons for being at Abner's club: pretty girls, gambling, and hunting. She hadn't understood what hunting had to do with Abner's club until later that evening when she overheard a conversation between the two men. Harry was hunting Abner Snow for crimes, including suspected murder, but he hadn't been able to make the charges stick. Nevertheless, Harry and Tori became friends, and it was Harry who got Tori her job with Galley Press.

Kale had met Abner and didn't care for him. Tori still insisted she liked him and could never imagine him as a criminal. Kale could, easily, and the thought of Abner buying Mary's church disturbed him. "The monks still own it for now, don't they?" he asked Bertie.

"Yes, of course. The monks haven't officially accepted his offer, but I heard they're going to. I can't really blame them for wanting to sell. They have never used it in any religious capacity. It's just a pile of rock to them. It was meant to be a church, but from the very beginning they used it as a place to squeeze juice for their jams and jellies. That is, until Mary Gant took it over."

"The Mad Monks of Mendelenham," Tori said, shaking her head, "still around, just like in Mary Gant's day. I can't bear to think the church might be sold away for a gambling house."

Bertie pulled the car to a stop in front of the Priory. "It won't be if I get my hands on some fast money."

Harry gripped the door handle then twisted around. "But that's the whole point here, isn't it, Bertie? If the party goes as planned, we'll beat Abner Snow to the punch and you can buy the place from under his greedy nose."

Kale pondered the implications. Bertie and Harry were definitely attaching some measure of loot to this Mary Mystery party. How did that tie into the dozen headless ladies from centuries past?

Missing heads, arson, mad monks, a half-wit monster from Bourton, and now the prospect of fast money and Abner Snow. The puzzle had grown, and Kale sensed a black cloud forming over the village of Wychwood. "Tori, this place is starting to give me the creeps," he whispered, and opened the car door.

Chapter Four

Kale lay sprawled across Tori's great square bed leafing through a copy of *Country Life* magazine. Warm sunlight fell across the room from the spread of windows, and only the occasional squabble of rooks from the church disturbed his thinking. Kale's occasional glance up at the portrait of Prioress Mary and her benevolent smile revealed where his thoughts really lay—searching for a motive. Nobody commits mass murder without a reason. There had to be one.

By four o'clock he'd finished Tori's entire supply of magazines and decided to have a nap. A few minutes later, from a half-sleep, he heard the door open behind him.

"Tori?"

No reply. He rolled over and propped his chin on a hand. There in the doorway stood a glowering black clad figure whose visage shocked him like a bucket of ice water. "Don't move," he cried, scrambled off the bed, and ran into his room, bare feet slapping the stone floor.

"It's me!" Tori laughed as she entered the room with a swish of her long black robe.

"I said don't move! I'm trying to find my camera." Kale had the bag half emptied before he remembered taking it in for repairs.

"Lousy luck!" he fumed, hating to miss the chance for such a remarkable photo. He turned and retraced his steps to where Tori now stood on the bed in exactly the same posture as her infamous relative.

"Well, what do you think? Peas in a pod? Bertie had this made by a London costumer." She ran her fingers along the rim of the scarf pressing into the flesh of her neck and cheeks. "This wimple is driving me crazy."

"It's unbelievable. You look identical." Kale stood hands on hips looking from the nun in the portrait back to Tori, grappling with the uncanny resemblance. It was more than just the black habit and the floppy hat. The wimple, wound about her head and hiding her thick hair, emphasized every feature of her face more fully. Her forehead, suddenly elongated, made her appear sterner. Her eyes, though still merry, appeared darker, deeper, and more mysterious. Her lips, like Mary Gant's, were full and passionate, if such a thing could be said of a nun. He realized if Tori frowned, she would be positively menacing, not the Tori he knew at all. The transformation seemed surreal. Tori even wore a silver neck chain with a dangling whistle. Everything matched . . . almost.

Kale stared at the portrait. Walking over to the bed, he hopped up and, standing face-to-face with Mary Gant, saw what the casual observer was sure to miss. Something else dangled on Mary's silver chain . . . something that took his breath away. A jewel—a huge faceted oval—skirted Mary's silver whistle like a picture frame. The painter had done good job, even disclosing tiny faces painted onto the facets of the stone like a mirrored reflection. He counted thirteen, twelve women and one man. "Who's the man, Tori?"

"Lord Caddington, one of Bertie's ancestors. He's the one who gave Mary the stone."

He suddenly understood the treasure hunt. He pointed to the portrait. "So that's what this is about!

"The Cavendish diamond!" Beaming from ear to ear, Lord Bertie strode through the door carrying a large silver tray. "Didn't Victoria tell you about it?"

Kale frowned and watched Tori flop backward onto the bed in a flounce of black robes and giggles. "No, she didn't! It must have slipped her mind. Listen, Bertie, you can't actually believe a stone like that would still be around here."

Bertie laughed. "They burned down your office, didn't they? That's a good sign it's still around."

Kale stared hard at him. Who would suspect Galley Press would have such a diamond? Surely Tulley's visit to the inn hadn't been in search of the treasure, had it?

"The Cavendish diamond weighed 114 carats and was liberated from the Turks by General Lord Cavendish. His heir and nephew, Lord Alexander Caddington, gave the stone to Mary Gant as collateral for a loan, actually. It disappeared during the tragedy and has not been seen since. Worth a king's ransom." He looked up longingly at Mary's portrait, shrugged, and set down his silver tray laden with a huge bowl of fresh raspberries. Beside the raspberries sat a dish of clotted cream so thick the spoon stood straight up. Two small booklets had been placed on the tray; Kale leaned over and fingered *Rules of Rummoli* and *Mary Gant's Journal.* Bertie looked on, smiling. "You will need to read them to better enjoy tomorrow's festivities." He plucked an invitation from his jacket pocket that bore the Bertillon family crest and requested their presence at his ancestral home for dinner: "The manor is just two miles down the road. I shall drive you."

Tori looked overjoyed.

"And, I have come bearing gifts," Bertie said quietly. From over his arm, he unfolded Kale's costume. "The trousers, tie, vest, and dickey front are new; the waistcoat is from our costume stock." After casting an appraising eye on Kale for proper fit, he nodded and laid it all on the bed. "The maid will bring your boots tomorrow, Kale."

"I'm a size 12D. American 12D."

"Of course you are. Harry Bass was good enough to tell me you favored a Church's shoe. I called them. Victoria helped me with your clothing sizes. I pray she was correct."

While Tori changed out of her Mary Gant guise, Kale picked up Bertie's five-page party booklet. "Rummoli? We're going to play a card game?"

"Precisely," Bertie said. "Very integral to the treasure hunt. Now, enjoy your raspberries; I must go and prepare for arrivals. It's all very exciting."

Kale moved to one of the antique wing chairs, sat, and flipped through pages of Bertie's rulebook. The first three listed the rather mundane rules of rummoli, a game that combined both poker and rummy with a playing board for betting. Kale remembered the game from summer camp. Any number of people could play; it only required extra decks of cards.

He skipped the rules and flipped to the last two pages that outlined events leading up to the nursery rhyme murders. Kale read how crafty Mary, along with her girls of the black habits, had come to Wychwood and refurbished the old monastery ostensibly for a priory, but in actuality as a weekend retreat for the Club of old Covent Gardens.

"Sounds like an American football club," Kale muttered to himself. He read it was an organization of dedicated beef-lovers. He turned to the last page, which contained a list of the steak club members and a very brief biography on each. Kale imagined them together, just a bunch of very rich good old boys looking to get out of the city for a little fun. Their sustained fame convinced Kale of the problems the authorities must have encountered investigating the demise of Mary and her girls. It would have meant questioning these very powerful club members.

On the back cover, Bertie or someone had sketched a seating diagram. Except for the item marked *pontificating chair,* it bore little interest. He tried to imagine how someone would be chosen for a pontificating chair. Perhaps lots were drawn, and while thick cuts of beef sizzled on the brazier, the drawer of the shortest stick entertained from the canopied pontificating chair.

"Must have been fun," he said to himself, thinking a bit more excitedly of the party and hoping the festivities would follow the lead of the original. The booklet ended with a mention of the dozen women being decapitated, and their bodies thrown into a fruit press. The deed done, the husks of their drained bodies had been carried up to the main floor and piled in front of the church podium; that same podium on which had been found the infamous clue, that centuries-old nursery rhyme. Kale stretched out across the bed, retrieved the booklet and reread the rhyme aloud: "Mary Mary quite contrary, how does your garden grow? With silver bells and cockleshells and pretty maids all in a row." It had a small line of credit about borrowing the rhyme from its Mary, Queen of Scots origins, but that didn't interest him. He was intrigued by the lack of punctuation in the rhyme and if Mary Gant actually had a garden, but dismissed the thought and decided that metaphor must have prompted people to link the old rhyme to the murders. The garden must have meant Mary's fruit supply, without which she couldn't make her brandy.

Then his eyes settled on the small black and white photo at the bottom of the page of an old liquor bottle that bore a credit to the Victoria & Albert Museum. He rolled closer to the bedside lamp and examined the image. The embosser on the bottle read *Wychwood Spirits,* and he noted that Bertie had written, *est. total production—one hundred thousand bottles per annum.* Kale whistled and wondered how the women managed to get that many bottles into the priory, let alone out again under the noses of the king's tax collectors.

Kale could smell a story. Excited, he grabbed the other booklet Bertie had placed on the tray, a copy of Mary Gant's journal. Not a daily account per se, rather her observations of Wychwood and about fifty pages of poetry. Kale began at the beginning. With every page, the woman became more of a reality. Mesmerized for an hour, and disappointed there was no mention of illegal liquor, he eventually leaned his head back upon the soft pillows and tried to imagine Wychwood in the time of Prioress Mary until he drifted to sleep.

In his dream, glass workers made and stacked jars and bottles, foresters hauled great oak logs, mill workers busily sawed, coopers made barrels by the hundreds, workers quarried ledge stone and roofing tiles, and drovers hauled everything away to the waiting barges. In the summer and fall months, he dreamed those same drovers worked double-time hauling wagons heaped with tender berries to the great press that Mary had designed and called *the beast*. Mary had included a small drawing of the beast in her journal. No measurements, just a little stick person to denote comparative size and a two-word explanation for its height: *filter tank*. No surprise, for on the previous page Mary had delved into the problems of finding a proper filter medium for the elixir and had given credit to "L" for coming up with a mixture of charcoal and grain chaff.

Kale awoke staring at the ceiling. Wychwood would

have been a bustling place, very different from the derelict town it was today. There could have been dozens of informants, he mused, and closed his eyes. Why hadn't the tax collector discovered the bottles? Had a search for the bottles been conducted and turned up only jam crocks? Bribed? Were the tax collectors paid off? No, the authorities would have suspected that and sent spies. The woman must have been a genius to have run an entire bottling business and not get caught.

Mary would have needed a whole countryside of fruit to fill one hundred thousand bottles. The stills must have run night and day. But where would she have kept those? Certainly the building would have been searched top to bottom.

Tori knocked and entered some time later. "Wake up, you silly bear."

"I'm awake. Just thinking."

"Be a dear and tell me what you've come up with. We're partners, remember."

"Humph. You didn't even tell me about the diamond. Some partner."

"Harry told me not to." Her smile was quick.

Kale rolled his eyes, "I was dreaming about dancing heads. Thirteen bloody heads with pleading bottle-cork eyes and big feet with clunky brown shoes."

"Do you think history may repeat itself? That an old crime will be revisited by the same people?"

Kale sat straight up. "Yes. But what's the motive?"

"My ancestor's missing diamond?"

"Good, but we obviously don't have it, so why torch our building? And it's not enough to massacre thirteen nuns. Yeah, I know, they weren't real nuns, but that didn't seem to bother anybody. Certainly a bunch of monks wouldn't have murdered them, and not over a diamond."

"Bertie said Mary took over the church and cut her ties with the monks; it's possible she cut them off their juice supply."

"I still don't buy that as a motive, not for a bunch of monks. The killings must have been by an outsider for some purpose."

"A warning?"

"To whom, Tori? And what kind of warning entails slaughtering defenseless women? Besides, the liquor business fell apart after the murders. Where would the benefit be in destroying their livelihood?"

"I don't know. Maybe there were some upstanding folks who figured out what Mary was up to and took offense to her mode of income."

"That makes no sense—a person put off by her liquor and antics, but up for slaughtering a dozen women? No. I think they must have been killed for something they all knew. Some common knowledge they all shared. They were killed to shut them up; it's the only reason that makes any sense. But what could it be? What did they have in common? What did all the women have in common besides being female?"

A new thought dawned on him as he stared at Tori, and his eyes grew wide.

"Kale, why are you looking at me like that?"

"I'm wondering how it is you're standing there? If Mary was disguised as a nun, how did she manage to procreate? If that was the case, then you wouldn't be here, would you?"

Tori laughed, "Now aren't you the astute observer. It's about time you twigged."

"Well?"

"Mary and Lord Caddington were lovers before she came to Wychwood. Some stories say they had a boy name William and had him raised by distant relatives.

"My great-granny tells a different story. Granny swears she has evidence Mary was truly a nun despite the stories about the elixir and Lord Caddington. She swears that at least at the end of her life Mary was with an order in America. According to Granny's story, there were two children—twins—and they weren't Mary's, but rather children of Mary's deceased twin: a boy and a girl. The boy was wild, drank heavily, and died young in a fight.

"Granny says Mary fostered them, and plied Lord Caddington with liquor to employ them in his household, right here in Wychwood under everyone's noses.

"Now, don't you feel bad for saying I've kept you in the dark? My heritage is all a huge family secret, kept as quiet as the family recipe for Christmas pudding."

Kale let her words turn over in his head. Secrets and recipes. The idea came to them both at the same time. "Recipes!" They both laughed, for the idea the women were slaughtered for a recipe sounded absurd.

Across the road, a truck engine started up. Kale and Tori walked to an open window and watched an old white truck pull out from the shadow of the church and squeak off up the north road toward Bourton.

Kale clasped Tori's hand and nodded toward the church. "That's where we need to go."

Tori nodded. "You're right. I bet there are clues galore."

Kale sighed as Tori pulled her hand away and headed out the door to tea. Tori never seemed to grasp how he felt about her.

Chapter Five

T hat evening, at precisely seven o'clock, Kale knocked on the connecting door and stepped into Tori's room. He'd donned a charcoal gray suit, a freshly starched white shirt, and around his neck hung the art deco tie his sister had sent him last Christmas. The first time he'd worn it Tori had squealed with delight and correctly predicted the others' reaction: Neddy almost spit out her tea, and the late Enoch Tulley stared for ten full seconds before clearing his throat and muttering something about Americans wearing their tastes around their necks. It had become a standing joke—Kale's American tie.

He stood in his doorway a moment staring at the vacant room, wondering if Tori had already gone down when he heard a noise in the dressing room: a thump, followed by a loud curse. As he headed for the commotion, the dressing room door opened and out she stepped, a vision in a long, clingy red satin gown, sleeveless and sleek. She looked more than sexy, more than alluring; she looked elegant. Hair pulled back, drop earrings decorating her ears, a pearl choker glimmering against the high neckline of her dress. "Wow!"

"Stubbed my toe," she said smiling and pointing back at the dressing room.

He nodded, mesmerized.

She held out a pair of red shoes. "I can't bend over to get these things on. Can you help me?"

He nodded again, and found sense enough to cross the room. As he crouched on the floor, she wriggled the satin up around her knees. Suddenly the position of shoe salesman seemed enviable. He took each leg lightly in his hand one at a time, and guided her feet into the red leather dress slippers. As she dropped the dress back into place, her smile appeared as dreamy as the moment. He felt he'd been given a taste of her, even though he'd seen her legs a thousand times.

"Come on, Yank. Bertie and Harry are waiting."

Tugged upright by his tie, Kale returned her impish grin. After a deep, calming breath, he took an arm and escorted her out the door.

Outside, Bertie leaned against his old Bentley. "Ah, there you are. Harry's begged off. He's studying some of my puzzle pieces. Nose to the grindstone, you might say."

Bertie ushered Tori into the front passenger seat. Kale slumped into the backseat, alone but happy.

Clouds obliterated the sky. Not dark enough for lights, the car rumbled up the main street where odd shadows stirred in the gloom and the howling of a dog broke the settled quiet.

The big car roared past the south bridge, crested a hill and entered the great Wychwood Forest. Low on the horizon, the sun lit the great oaks a golden color. Kale stared out the open window entranced by the sheer number and size of the mighty trees.

"This is heaven," murmured Tori, and made Bertie slow the Bentley to a crawl.

A mile or so down the narrow road, Bertie came to a near stop and turned the car a hard right through a break in an impossibly tall yew hedge onto a drive lined with huge oak trees on both sides. A narrow track led off to the left and disappeared into the shrubbery.

Tori peered out the window, "What's up there?"

"A small version of Stonehenge called the Roll Round Stones, for reasons that would be obvious if you saw them. As a small boy I used to creep through the forest and watch the Druids for hours. It's a full moon tonight. Perhaps you'd like to go spy on them? There's usually a few hanging around."

"Druids?" asked Kale.

"Yes, like at Stonehenge."

"You can't be serious. That's folklore."

"It certainly is not. They were priests of their time before Christianity. Much farmland in these parts was owned by Celts, and each tribe held their own territories and practiced their old religion with ancient rituals. It may seem odd to a Yank, but ancient history is alive and well in our land, especially by a full moon."

Tori focused her attention straight ahead. "Sounds like fun, but not tonight."

Bertie chuckled and accelerated the car.

With the Roll Round Stones behind them, Kale leaned over the seat to whistle his admiration. Wreathed in ground mist and settled dead center in a bowl-shaped pasture sat Bertillon Manor.

Elizabethan in style, the great house boasted two wings running east and west from a connecting round tower of surprisingly different color and construction. Tall windows graced the entire fronts of both wings.

"Bertie, your house is wonderful," Tori cooed. "Like a page from a fairy tale, and so, so white."

Bertie sighed, "It's simply the moonlight on the limestone. My ancestors couldn't bring themselves to build with slate. Too common a stone. She's too big, a bugger to heat, impossible to maintain, and can be yours for a paltry sum. I've been trying to sell it for years. Twenty bedrooms and a very leaky roof." The car jerked into a pothole and continued forward. "Not all the rooms are functional. In fact, a goodly number of them are in ruin."

"Ruin?"

"The leaky roof. It's been a sieve for generations." Bertie parked the car beside a small portico just to the left of the tower and escorted them to a front door that opened into a great hall complete with draped flags and a suit of armor in every corner. Black and white tiles had replaced yesteryear's floor, while overhead a huge chandelier cast a romantic light over the length of a long banquet table. On their right, a wide, maroon carpeted staircase led up to a balustrade walk-around that reminded Kale of an Italian courtyard. The contrast in times was startling and very effectively enhanced the historical feeling of the space. The innermost wall featured a movie set fireplace big enough to cook an elephant.

"Basil Rathbone," Tori whispered, "the fireplace in the old Robin Hood movie."

Kale nodded, but he couldn't take his eyes off the glittering suits of armor, each holding a different weapon.

From a wide doorway on their left, a man appeared. Decked out in formal wear, he bowed slightly and said, "Good evening, milord. Cook is awaiting instructions."

"Thank you, Edwin. These are my friends Miss Roche and Mister Kale. We'll be in momentarily."

"Very good, sir."

Kale had never seen a real live butler, and it gave him a momentary thrill. But after Edwin had gone from the doorway, Bertie said, "Edwin is only here for tonight, he comes along with Bridgett the cook. Explore later, Victoria," Bertie said pulling Tori away from a wall tapestry toward the wide doorway. Kale dropped the face flap on the suit of armor he was inspecting and hurried to catch up.

For all the rough sparseness of the great hall, the living room looked lush and inviting. Light oak floors waxed to a sheen, faded rose-colored wallpaper, gleaming tables, and lots of overstuffed chairs. The high walls supported huge landscape paintings and lots of small renditions of fat pigs and placid, block-shaped bulls. Eccentric lamps, odd statues, and knickknacks from generation upon generation of Bertillons lay scattered about like icons of past family life.

Tori's demeanor fell to a look of earnest coveting, and Kale couldn't help but smile. Exploring, he picked up a red-coated toy soldier from a complete set on a corner table and examined the fine details of the casting. Reluctantly, he placed it back in the ranks and turned to watch Tori flit around the room, entranced and excited. She turned his way with a raised eyebrow, and he knew she had thoughts of buying this Elizabethan white elephant. A pile of rotting stones with a fancy name had to be the last thing two people with a struggling business needed, but he had to admit, the place was intriguing.

"Come, come," Bertie called from the end of the room, "this way, it's quicker. We mustn't keep Bridgett waiting. She gets angry as a bear when food gets cold."

They crossed a wide hallway into a study fitted out with leather wing chairs and a huge oak desk. Kale loved the book walls and wanted to peruse the volumes, but Bertie wagged a finger and led them on into a music room that contained only a grand piano, an old harp, and a few dozen buckets still standing with water from the last rain.

"Darn roof." Bertie shook his head and trudged onward to another hallway, down past two closed doors and into the great hall . . . back where they had started. Kale wondered if Bertie ever showed his guests anything other than the most confusing route. He wondered where the butler had gone to; if anyone needed a proper full-time butler, it was Bertie.

As they passed by the door of a small kitchen, Bertie hailed the white-coated cook, who stood looking plump and nonplussed.

"We're ready, my dear," he said.

He held open a swinging door and ushered Kale and Tori into a private dining room, more intimate than the great hall, but no less impressive. Wall sconces shaped like torches cast a shifting light over the carved claw-footed table and chairs. Tori gushed over the embroidered chair seats, each portraying a different scene from the *Iliad.*

"Fascinating," Kale whispered, becoming ever more charmed as he took his seat. He realized they could never come close to affording the place, and even if they could, the repairs would cost a fortune. Fixing only the roof would be way beyond their means.

Bridgett served a divine dinner of baked trout that her husband Edwin had caught in the Evenlode River. The river, according to Bertie, marked all but the southern boundary of his property. By the time dessert arrived, a steamed sponge cake with toffee sauce, Tori had absorbed every tidbit of history offered by Bertie, and Kale had become suspicious of her intentions.

After the meal, they went through the kitchen into the Great Hall. "I have saved the best for last," Bertie announced. "This way to the Norman keep." Bertie guided them across the Great Hall and down into the corner where a narrow, short passage led into the round tower. Constructed of rough-split slate, the tower walls supported a scary looking stairway that corkscrewed up and up and out of sight. Armor and weapons lined the walls and the scene overpowered any shred of resistance in Kale. As if challenging his resistance, a stuffed armored warhorse stood dead center, ready to charge.

Bertie pointed up at the catwalk crossing far above their heads and told them it connected the hallway of both wings. "I installed that after the last fire took out the only remaining floor and the remains of the south wing. That portion was destroyed by fire three times over the centuries. I wasn't about to rebuild it again. The east and west wings are headache enough."

Bertie returned them to the hotel at midnight. In the empty lobby they paused and listened to a clock strike the hour. Tori began twirling around and around in time to each gong and at the last one came to a dizzying stop in Kale's grasp. Her breath was warm upon his cheek.

She whispered, "Will you do something for me?"

"Anything, anything at all."

"Then help me buy Bertillon Manor."

"Are you kidding?" he said, stepping back and flopping into a lobby chair. "That's as likely to happen as the two of us finding Mary's diamond."

"But that's exactly what we're going to do. Time to start the hunt. Let's go." She ran for the steps and ascended them as quickly as the satin gown would allow.

Ten minutes later, changed into jeans, dark sweaters, and armed with a flashlight found on a dressing room shelf, the pair tiptoed down the stairs and out the front door into the dark of night. Quickly they padded down the hotel walk and beelined across the car park and street to the weedy edge of the churchyard.

"Are you sure you want to do this?" Kale asked, his voice hushed for fear of stirring the dead.

"Of course not, but I won't let anyone beat me to that stone."

"Tori, I don't believe there is a diamond. Not after all these years. This is crazy. I think we should go back."

Thunder cracked and a flash of lightning lit up the churchyard like the set of a horror movie. Tori screamed and rain gushed from the sky. Kale reached out, clasped her hand, and together they dashed up the neglected walkway to the shelter of the church portico.

Kale squeezed Tori's hand for reassurance, passed her the light, and reached with both hands for the door latch. It didn't give easily. Two, three weighty tugs and the heavy door finally scraped against the slate entrance and swung open. He stepped into the tiny vestibule containing a dried up Holy water font, a staircase to a choir loft perhaps, and two tall, narrow doors. He beckoned for Tori, clasped her hand, and passed through the open double doors into a carnival of colored light.

Stained glass windows set high up and at four- or five-foot intervals surrounded the entire room and turned the staccato lightning flashes into a riot of blue and blood-red lights. Rain flooded in through holes in the roof and pattered on the floor like a wild echoing drumbeat. The sanctuary had been stripped. Even the pews, if they'd ever been in place, had been removed, leaving the space wide open.

"May I have this dance," Kale kidded.

Tori smiled nervously. "That lightening was close. We could have been killed, and you joke."

"It's from playing golf. American boys are taught the fine points of avoiding electrocution before puberty. Don't hide under a tree, don't open your umbrella, and never, ever scream because it brings on the rain."

Tori cast the beam around the scarred plaster walls. Raised alcoves, which had been designed for the tabernacle and statues of saints, accommodated birds' nests. Spiderwebs hung like silver threads in every corner.

Kale took the light and stepped forward with Tori behind, their footsteps echoing in the hollow space. Together they moved across the floor and up two steps to the podium. There it was, now too obscured to read, but trusted to be the nursery rhyme scrawled by the murderers hundreds of years before.

Lightning flashed and created colored monsters in their minds, followed by another loud clap of thunder.

"Come on," Tori said, pulling him back toward the entrance. But she didn't intend to leave. Reaching the vestibule, she opened one of the two narrow doors revealing a tiny cloakroom, and inside that, another even narrower door. "It's locked. Help me look for the key."

Kale felt along the doorjamb and a bookshelf off to the side, but couldn't find a key. "How did you know this door was here?"

"Bertie told me. It leads to the cellar. And of course I want to go in. It may be the secret hiding place of Mary's treasure."

Thunder shook the building and her face flashed open and frightened in front of him. "Size twelve's are as good as a key any day." Kale leaned back and gave the door a swift kick, then led the way into the musty stairwell, cautiously testing each downward step. At the bottom, he turned and took the light from Tori. "Amazing. It looks like nothing has changed since that last day."

"Bertie told me no one has ever been down here," Tori whispered. "They're afraid of being cursed by the dead women."

Against the far wall, the beam of light hit upon the wood slats of the infamous fruit press . . . Mary Gant's beast. It rose up like a water tower and almost touched the ceiling. Kale thought the top part looked similar to ones he'd seen used by winemakers in his hometown of Riverside, Michigan. In modern versions, motors screwed down the metal plate that sent the rivers of juice gushing between the slats. He couldn't determine what drove the plate into this beast.

After a moment's hesitation, Kale headed off in that direction. Slowly they picked their way between crates and tables, and around streams of rainwater seeping through the sanctuary floorboards. Kale reached the press first and put his hand on the ancient machine.

Tori gasped and pointed up to ribs of the great press. "That's blood! And that looks like dried—" Thunder reverberated around them, cutting off her words, but not her meaning.

Rain pattered onto the floor in various spots, leaking from the room above. Their eyes met, sickened at the reality of what had once flowed out from the wooden slats.

"I can smell it, Kale."

"All right, that's it for me. Let's get out of here."

As they bustled back through the clutter, Tori slipped on a patch of wet slate and fell. Bending over to help her, Kale lit up the floor with the light and saw water circulating around a crack in the slate pavers. He bent lower and put his ear almost to the floor.

"Tori! Listen to this." He pointed to the crack in the floor.

She bent, listened a moment, and understood immediately. "It's too much water for a storm drain. It must be an underground stream, perhaps off the Evenlode. It must have run the press."

Kale listened again to the torrent below. "I'll bet it flows under the Priory. There must be an access there and down here, somewhere."

Tori grinned. "What a convenient way to transport barrels and cases of liquor. Plunk them in and let the river carry them downstream."

"That would certainly explain why the king's tax men couldn't find anything."

"Interesting, but it doesn't tell us where the diamond is."

A thunderclap shook the building. Tori jumped and bumped a crate, which in turn knocked over another and sent a rat scrambling across her feet. Tori screamed and ran for the steps like a singed cat. Kale laughed and loped away after her, not catching up until they were across the road and headed for the safety of the Priory.

The rain had stopped. An almost full moon blazed silver at the scudding clouds. From somewhere down the street, an animal howled like a wolf. Kale shivered with apprehension.

Chapter Six

Early the next morning, a piercing scream shot Kale bolt upright in his bed.

"Tori!" Kale rolled onto the floor wearing only his boxer shorts and ran into her room ready for anything, except Harry.

"What are you doing here?"

Harry couldn't get the grin off his face. "Wait now, it's not what you think. I didn't mean to end up in here. A messenger arrived from London with a package. I gave him a spot of tea in the kitchen and decided to take the secret passage back to my room, but lost my way. That door was open."

Tori knelt on the bed with the comforter wrapped around her body. Only her head showed.

"You should have knocked, Harry," she said.

"Bloody right; your scream took a year off my life."

"You scared me right out of bed, Harry." Tori yelled.

Gripping the comforter around her, she slipped from the bed with a soft thud, "Harry, stop grinning." Tori stomped her foot hard and went trailing away to her dressing room.

"I'm sorry, but I didn't know it was your room," Harry called after her. "I just blundered in. That secret passageway is dark as sin and the door was open. I—"

"That is hardly a secret passageway, Harry. Bertie shows it to everybody."

"You're right. Bertie thinks the passages are the key to finding Mary's diamond. The poor guy has spent himself dry trying to find new passageways. Got hisself convinced there's a way across to the old church and is hoping somebody will stumble onto it."

Tori turned at the dressing room door and exchanged knowing looks with Kale. So far, they must be the only ones who had happened on the underground stream.

Harry continued. "Anyway, if you don't want people using this door, don't leave it open. I'd have never found it, otherwise."

The conspiratorial gleam between Kale and Tori died; they hadn't opened the door. Somebody other than Harry must have been opened it.

Tori gasped. "Whoever it was has been through every drawer and all my clothes." She slammed the dressing room door.

Kale retreated to his room for trousers. Harry followed, leaning in the doorway. "That messenger from London had some information about your fire. And some info about another matter, one a little closer to home. It concerns the late Enoch Tulley."

Kale didn't want to hear anything incriminating about his deceased boss. "If it's about his delinquent taxes, I'm not interested." Trousers zipped, shirt buttoned, he shoved past Harry into the main suite and flopped into a wing chair to wait for Tori. He wanted Harry to leave.

Harry followed. "The arsonists tried to open that hidden wall safe in Tulley's office. They botched the job. The fire investigators called in CID."

"My office," Kale reminded him, "at least it was."

Tori called from her dressing room. "We could never get in that safe. Did the arsonists blow it up? I remember Tully saying it was top of the line and fireproof."

"It was the best, a Gibraltar number 5, and no, they didn't get it open. CID got it open."

"Was there anything in the safe?"

"Only this!" Harry bent down, opened his satchel, and withdrew a tin letterbox. He handed it over to Kale.

"Whatever it is, wait for me," Tori yelled.

Kale wasn't about to wait. He opened the box and found the inside stuffed with pages of old parchment and a dozen or so folded paper squares. Some bore the words *Leviticus, at Bourton,* in very bold script, while others bore the words *free, for Caddington,* in a lighter, more flowing script.

Tori pranced from the dressing room fully clothed with a shock of red lipstick and hair somewhat wilder than usual, barely brushed and falling unrestrained to her shoulders. Her blue plaid skirt, short and pleated, flipped with each step. More attracting to the eye was her yellow Shetland sweater. It clung to everything.

"Let me see," she said.

She took one look at the papers and pronounced the first page a recipe. She leafed through them all, counting as she went. "Thirty-one, and they all look like recipes for liquor. As dumb as the idea of stolen recipes sounds, seems we were right about what the murdered girls had in common."

Kale said nothing. He sat stunned, wondering why the business had been burned over something as simple as recipes.

Tori identified the small folded squares as stationery. "Letters. People didn't have envelopes in those days, they simply folded the paper and sealed it with wax." She took one, and carefully opened it to reveal a blank page. She turned it over and guessed the words *Leviticus, at Bourton,* had been penned by Mary Gant. "It looks exactly like my writing." Then she hazarded another guess that the stationery had been supplied to Mary for easy posting to the abbot. "Don't you remember? Bertie told us that Leviticus was the perpetual name of the abbot monk of Mendelenham? There has been an Abbot Leviticus at the Bourton Monastery since just after Norman times."

"Kale, hide this one away somewhere safe." Harry reached in and carefully drew another paper from the very bottom of the box. Older than the others, it still bore half a section of blood-red sealing wax, bits of which crumbled off in his hand.

He held his breath as Harry carefully opened the ancient document. The hand-wrought gold and magenta border illustrations brought a gasp of delight from Tori.

"Why, it's beautiful. Here, let me see it. I studied Latin in school." She carefully took the parchment from Harry's hands. "It's a religious charter; a franchise, and there's a formula of some kind . . . a medicine perhaps." She translated the long list of herbs and spices aloud and was only stuck on the meaning of one word—*caligolignum.* "The literal translation is "dizzy wood," but I don't know what that is."

Kale was more interested in the little blue note tacked to the bottom edge: *Lifted from the records at Mendelenham.* There was a date posted beneath it. "See that date, Tori? That's three days before Tulley's accident."

Tori blanched, "Harry, was Tulley murdered?"

Harry shrugged, pulled out a cell phone, and began tapping numbers as he moved to the bowl of strawberries on the table. A dozen berries went down like clockwork as he talked on the phone. When finished his conversation Harry shoved the phone back into his pocket with berry-stained fingers.

"Put that page somewhere safe, Kale. I'll be back shortly." He headed for the fireplace and the secret entrance but halfway in he stopped and turned around. "You ought to put something heavy up against this panel."

Kale looked back at the paper. "What is dizzy wood? Do you know?"

Tori concentrated. "I think it's another name for the hallucinogenic herb wormwood. French distillers used it in that liquor they called absinthe. Quite a popular beverage until it was banned. It's half the formula; one drink and you'd be silly for a week."

"That's not the half of it," Harry muttered and ducked into the hole like a rabbit.

Kale didn't like that comment and ran to the secret entrance yelling, "Harry! Harry! What did you mean by that? What do you know that you're not telling us?"

"I'm not sure," Harry called back. "Just put something extra heavy against that panel."

Tori stood forlorn, arms drooped. For the first time ever, she looked as if she needed someone. "I'm frightened, Kale. What if they're coming for us?"

"Help me push this desk against that panel."

She didn't move. "I'm beginning to see it now, Kale. We're in the middle of something big here. Bigger than we know. Want to bet Harry comes back and tells us he has to go off to London to see a man about a horse? That's always his story when he goes off investigating. And he does too. I mean, he actually does go and talk to men about horses. He's got dozens of them stashed in Ireland. You've never been to his place in Ireland, have you?"

"Quit talking and push."

With the barricade erected to their satisfaction, Kale retreated to his room to shower and throw on some jeans, a polo shirt, and moccasins. He emerged from his room in time to catch the end of a conversation between Harry and Tori.

"I'll be back later this afternoon, love," he said. "I have to go into the city and see a man about a horse." He winked at Kale on his way past.

"Told you," she said. They went to the window to watch Harry departing on his own agenda.

Across the road the sound of hammering exploded a flight of noisy rooks, birds that Tori and every true blue Englishman held dear to their hearts.

"Noisy, filthy crows," he teased.

Too fixated on the hammering, Tori failed to rise to the jibe. Kale leaned on the stone windowsill and followed her gaze to where a lone figure sat pounding away on the church roof. "Hermes Wheems, I presume."

"That's very odd," Tori whispered. "When you said his name he stopped pounding and looked this way— almost as if . . ."

Tori turned from the window, ran across the room, and began searching the drawers of the antique writing desk. Extracting a pen and paper, she wrote furiously.

Kale ambled over to the fireplace and read her note: *Go to the window, say nothing, just watch Wheems!*

Back at the window, Kale watched Wheems shatter slate with every hammer blow; he looked like a good worker.

Over by the desk, Tori tested out her suspicion. "Kale," she said, loudly, "let's go across to the church and find out what that Hermes Wheems knows."

Stunned, Kale watched Wheems suddenly throw down his hammer and scrabble down off the roof like a monkey.

"Tori, he heard us! There's a bug in this room."

It wasn't hard to find. She saw it on the underside of the lampshade. She snatched it off and headed toward the door. "Come on, let's get him."

Kale rounded into the hall running, but Tori had already gone down one flight. He was on the stairs, but she had gone down two flights. At the second, with two flights to go, Kale heard Bertie call, "Victoria, what's wrong?" and heard the front door slam back on its hinges.

Kale hit the bottom running hard for the door. Bertie was there, leaning out and calling after Tori. Kale almost bowled him over.

Tori stood on the road waving her arms and running for the white truck roaring out from behind the church. She ran like an antelope. Kale bent his head and ran faster than he ever had before, heart pounding, muscles complaining.

Wheems' truck sped through a side gate in the church wall, skidded sideways, and raced up the narrow lane toward the road.

Panting, lungs screaming for air, Kale saw the girl of his dreams leap to the top of the wall and jump, and land like a rag doll.

"Tor-iiii!"

Chapter Seven

Kale found her sitting in the long grass, fixing her hair.

"I've lost my hair ribbon. Can you help me find it?" she said, springing to her feet.

He'd pictured her maimed, if not run over by the wacky Wheems, and she wanted help finding her hair ribbon! "What were you thinking? You could have been killed."

She stood there dusting off her clothes. "Really Kale, you oughtn't worry so much. I just wanted to talk to him. How was I supposed to know he wouldn't stop? I almost had him. I was into the back of his truck, but then he hit a hole and out I went. Lucky the ground is soft."

"And what if he hadn't hit the ditch? He wouldn't have stopped. He would have gone on to Bourton with you in the back." He turned and walked off, but after a

68

few steps he spotted the ribbon, picked it up, and returned to hand it to her without a word.

"Come on, Kale, don't be miffed," she laughed. "I've lost his bugging device too. I meant to throw it at him. I hope there aren't any more of those things."

Kale turned his back and strode off toward the Priory. How could she scare him like that and then laugh about it? It was all too much. By the time he reached the hotel door he was so puffed up with anger that pausing to assure Bertie she was uninjured was a chore.

Bertie nodded, "Of course she's all right. You just have to look at the girl to tell she's a natural athlete. But why in the world was she trying to stop Hermes Wheems?"

Kale shrugged and walked on through the open doorway.

"I have lunch ready for the both of you on the patio," Bertie called after him.

"You eat with her. I've had enough," Kale yelled, and continued striding through the reception area and dining hall to the rose garden. His bruised ego mingled with the heady essence of the flora and his almost palpable anger.

He toured the garden area, plucked a flower, and held it to his nose. It made him feel better. He continued on to the old shed at the edge of the garden.

The door creaked open at his touch, and a damp, earthy odor enveloped him. The lack of windows made him blind to everything but tools and the odd bit of garden stuff. Shovels, rakes, pruning shears, and a tumble of pots and bags of peat were piled against the wall. He opened the door a bit more and the light gleamed upon a tool like the one carried by the grim reaper—a scythe. Kale had never seen one. He took a step toward the wicked-looking instrument.

"Here, what you want in my shed?" came a deep rasping from the darkest corner.

Kale stepped closer to see who was talking, but to no avail; the man's face remained hidden.

"I'm sorry. I didn't mean to disturb you. I was just poking about. You must be Potter, the gardener."

"Now ain't you a sharpie. I got no time for entertaining hotel guests. Best you be moving along."

Kale shrugged, glanced again at the scythe—such a deadly looking thing—and backed out. He would have preferred a better look at that rude gardener, but from his voice, he managed to conjure up an image of a long-bearded, pointy-eared garden gnome eating raspberry jam. Kale laughed to himself, wondering where the image of raspberries had come from. Then he realized he smelled raspberry. *Probably some odd English fertilizer,* he thought.

He took his time walking back through the garden, pausing again at the Confessor Rose—perfect, and likely very hard to maintain.

Voices wafted from the patio. Tori sat eating lunch with Bertie. She was just like the Confessor Rose—thorny, beautiful, and high maintenance.

He followed the path up to the patio and cast her a final slicing cut of his eyes.

The effort brought a response. She plied him with a smile, came over and took his hand. "I didn't mean to worry you by chasing off after Wheems. Come on. Please don't stay mad. Have something to eat; it will make me seem a bit less horrible. The ploughman's lunch is excellent. Have it with ham, it's local, and the cheeses are yummy. And they have real dill pickles."

Over her shoulder he saw Bertie twiddling his mustache and pretending indifference.

Kale tried to remain serious. He certainly wouldn't let Bertie see him blathering like a schoolboy. "That Wheems fellow could be dangerous. You ought to know better than to go chasing after him."

She pulled her hand away, stuck out her tongue, and laughed. Kale laughed too, and flagged a waitress. He ordered the ploughman's lunch with extra ham and listened to Bertie relate more history of the Priory.

"It's always been an inn of one sort or another. Nobody can be given full credit for its construction. Bits and pieces really, and by almost everybody; Romans, Saxons, Normans, monks, Mary Gant, they all had a hand. Oh, and we mustn't forget the Germans. Those buggers blew a hole in the roof, twice."

That tweaked Kale's curiosity, "How—"

"From a Zeppelin in 1916, and a Heinkle in '41. The place had been left to rot for twenty years before I decided to renovate." He prattled on, supplying the step-by-step details of the restoration.

Kale pretended to be attentive, but his thoughts were on Hermes Wheems and how he'd been spying on them. Who had put him up to it? And what did he expect to discover? He caught Tori looking at him intermittently and figured she could tell his mind was elsewhere. At Bertie's first pause, she leaned forward and touched his arm, "I really am sorry for chasing after Wheems, but just the thought of him seeing me in bed and listening to our conversation was maddening. I didn't really want to talk to him. I really wanted to stop him so you could give him a good drubbing."

That meant a million to Kale, but he wouldn't let her know how it affected him. He met her gaze, smiled, pulled up his chair and bit into the best dill pickle he'd ever tasted. Looking at Bertie, he asked, "Is Wheems dangerous?"

Irritated at the change in topic, Bertie shrugged and reached for a carrot stick. "I really hadn't considered Hermes Wheems involved in any shenanigans. He never struck me as capable of foul deeds. Too thick in the head, I would think."

"Perhaps it's just his appearance," Tori said, fingering her empty glass.

Bertie beat Kale to the bottle by a mile. "I think you're wrong about Wheems. He's a very capable roof man. He did the hotel roof. Did a fine job too. Only wish I could afford him at the manor. Harmless fellow, really."

Kale had another question, "Does this hotel have a cellar?"

"If it does, nobody has found it. I've looked, my father tried, my grandfather too. Looking drove that fine old gentleman into an institution. There is a cellar of sorts under the tower at the manor. If you hammer on the floor you can tell it's hollow. Nobody has ever found a way down. As to a cellar here in the hotel, I've pounded every inch of the floor and found nothing. We even had a mining engineer poking about on weekends. I had rather high hopes he would find a passage to the church, but that fellow gave up and took off to Fiji. There should be one though; they had to get the slate from somewhere.

"Do you mind if we take a look?"

"My dear boy, that is precisely why you are here. Search away."

With a nod from Bertie, Kale poured Tori another glass of wine and helped himself to more tea. One of them had to be cold sober, and despite appearances of being totally capable, he knew Tori felt vulnerable. A bit of indulgence might do her some good. He doubted she would sleep tonight knowing somebody, probably Hermes Wheems, had been roaming around in her bedroom.

As if he were reading minds, Bertie said, "I'll have that door bolted shut straight away, Victoria." Then he leaned on the table toward Kale. "I say, all this calls for further study of the tunnels. There must be a way to get in here without being seen. How else could Wheems, or whoever it was, get in? The Priory is like a fortress."

"There's more than one way to skin a wet cat," Tori whispered.

"How's that?" Bertie asked.

But before she could reveal anything of the underground stream, the sky darkened and let loose a downpour that sent them racing to the open door of the dining room.

"Lord Bertillon," called a stick of a man dressed in

chef's whites. "Tonight's party menu, sir. You will want to check it over."

Bertie waved Kale and Tori on ahead. "Go up and examine my passage map and explore a bit."

Kale headed toward the lobby, intending to go around to the tiny door that led up the back stairs to the passages.

"Go through the kitchen, a much more interesting way," Bertie called out.

Kale laughed, wondering when Bertie ever followed the easy path, but then a thought struck him. He spun around and headed for the kitchen. Running water and garbage clicked together in his mind. "Bertie, would you mind if we gave the kitchen the once-over?"

"Not at all," replied the chef. "By all means, pop in and have a good look-see."

Embarrassed, Kale nodded his appreciation. He should have asked both the chef and the owner. But then, what did he know of culinary ethics?

As if realizing Kale's quest was not just culinary curiosity, Bertie said, "Don't mind the new amenities. We've added a few things, but all else is just as it was in Mary's day. When they built the Priory in 1240, that kitchen doubled as a slaughterhouse. Prioress Mary redesigned everything, including that charcoal brazier."

Kale knew that from reading Mary's journal. A slaughterhouse would have lots of bones and gristle. An underground stream would have made a convenient garbage disposal. Now, if only he had a divining rod.

Preceding Kale, Tori stopped to grimace at her distorted reflection in the polished steel of the kitchen door. "Kale, will you like me when I'm old and fat like my reflection?"

"Not a chance."

She tossed her hair and paraded into the kitchen with an exaggerated swing of her hips.

Because Mary Gant had taken such efforts to convert the cavernous slaughterhouse into a kitchen worthy of hosting Club weekends, she had described the kitchen in detail in her journal.

In the center of the stone room stood a huge oak worktable. Twelve feet in length, it looked scarred and worn from long use. Either the table had been replaced with a copy, or indeed, this was the very slaughterhouse table scrubbed down by Mary's girls. Of a more recent issue, copper-bottomed pots hung from hooks overhead. Four slate washtubs, plumbed and caulked, and obviously from the nearer century, took up a good portion of one wall.

Tori walked past the table and washtubs to check the contents of the kitchen's two refrigerators. "Mmmm, quail for supper. I can't wait."

"You just ate!" Kale said, as he bent down to examine a wooden crate full of odds and sods.

"But, you said you'd love me when I'm old and fat."

"I did not." Kale looked up and saw her peering into the refrigerator. "Tori, even eating a hundred quail wouldn't make you fat. I just don't know how you can think of food after all we've eaten in the past two days."

"It will be different tonight. There'll be other guests vying for these birds. I'll ask Bertie to put a few away for later."

"No doubt he'll tag them with your name: Victoria R."

She twisted around. "Don't call me that, Mr. Joseph Bently Kale."

"Of course not," he muttered. "Only Lord Bertie has that privilege."

"I heard that," she said, rubbing a green apple on her skirt and biting into it. "It's different with Bertie."

"I know. I know." She had different rules for every man she met. He didn't stand a chance of ever figuring her out. But it didn't dull his attempts to.

He stood and surveyed the room. "Something's not the same here."

"That makes a lot of sense coming from someone who's never set foot in this room before."

He ignored the chance at a comeback and walked toward the charcoal brazier. He stopped and stepped back to admire the simplicity of Mary's design. Stroking his chin with one hand, he wondered if the woman had studied geometry, for it was a rather lovely half-hemisphere set upon a square block. The big, slate fire bowl looked all polished and black while the square block looked dull as chalkboard; he found the contrast striking. In his sophomore year at Yale he had monitored a semester of Renaissance culture that had included medieval cookery. He remembered the professor had made careful notation of the problems encountered in dispersing smoke and fumes in early kitchens. He had specifically mentioned the brazier, and the failed attempts at using the fireplace for venting. He recalled his mention of the success early cooks had of employing a cloth canopy and telescoping tube for transporting smoke and hot air, what he'd called a "caterpillar." This brazier had been adapted recently to vent through a fan and exhaust system. He bent to examine the brazier's footings. Nothing out of the ordinary, just a big square of heavy slate sitting flat on the floor, and judging by the grunge along the bottom edges it hadn't moved for centuries. That is, if it could move at all.

Kale placed his size-twelve shoe on the bottom of the four-foot diameter base and pushed. It wouldn't budge. Looking inside the bowl, he saw it had been freshly stoked with charcoal for tonight's banquet. Except for its obvious heavy weight and size, the iron-cooking grill looked normal enough. He put his hand on it and set the thing in motion, one very slow revolution. Amazed that such a heavy weight should turn so easily, he began removing charcoal from the center until he had exposed an axle. He hadn't expected otherwise, but to see one that was five inches wide invited closer inspection. Kale took the room key from his pocket and tapped on the iron axle. It rang like a hollow pot. He looked straight up and saw a hook in the ceiling. "Ingenious woman!"

"Why, thank you," Tori said.

"Not you. Your late, great, great grandma."

He spun the grill again and observed the axle's movement, a tiny puff of charcoal dust emanated from the worn gap between axle and slate. Again he pushed the grill, and again there was a tiny puff of charcoal dust.

"Curiouser and curiouser," he whispered, and got down on all fours. He would need a flashlight and a bucket of water, and was about to call out for Tori to find both when he spotted brown, crêpe-soled shoes coming toward him. He stood up quickly and found the shoes belonged to a dumpy young girl in trousers and apron. After a sharp look, she got busy hauling down pots and pans.

"Sorry, miss, we'll get out of your way."

He grabbed Tori by the elbow and hustled her up the hall, past the back staircase and toward the reception.

Tori tugged back, "Let's go up the passageway. We can examine Bertie's map of the passages."

"No time for that. I've got to think through something—something I just saw."

They paused at the steps, noticing a change around them. During the short span of time between lunch and their kitchen tour, the Priory had sprung to life. They abandoned the stairs and headed into a lobby that had become a wonderland adorned with dozens of pots of roses from the garden. It smelled divine. Adding to the charm were three old-world-garbed receptionists, all waiting to greet new arrivals and assist with their baggage. Miss Jenkins curtsied.

Through open doors at the right of the stairway, they spied Bertie's taproom with its black polished bar. Tori clasped Kale's hand and pulled him through the doors toward a smiling barman. A cordial enough fellow, all belly, and sporting a mustache equal in size and limpness to Bertie's. Nodding happily, he quickly filled Tori's request for two bottles of ice cold Moet Chandon and four drinking straws.

"I'm not drinking today," Kale advised.

"Good, more for me." She walked out sipping one and swinging the other by a finger.

Kale shook his head. The midnight prowler had shaken her up big-time.

Out in the reception area, the first guests had arrived and stood at the desk talking with Bertie.

"Victoria," Bertie hailed, "I have somebody I want you to meet."

Tori walked over. Kale dragged behind.

"Victoria Roche, and J. B. Kale, let me present Abner Snow and Mrs. Loretta Snow, my neighbors from across the river."

"Ex-Mrs. Snow," corrected the hourglass-figured bleached blond. Extending her hand to Kale, she repeated her first name slowly in syllables, "Lo-rett-aaaa."

Tori held up her arms in a shrug, both hands occupied with champagne bottles. "Hello, Loretta. Abner, it's so nice to see you again."

Bertie looked ecstatic, "Oh, so you do know each other. How jolly,"

Loretta smiled like a Hollywood starlet and eyed Tori's champagne. "Oh, Abner, do get me the same. With a straw please. It looks like fun."

Kale nodded politely to the couple and headed up the stairs to his room. *Abner Snow,* the man Harry suspected of being a murderer was trying to buy Mary's church. Why?

Kale wasn't alone with his thoughts for long. Within the hour, the door opened and in staggered Tori, leaving the door wide open behind her.

"What are you doing here?" he asked.

She spun around, her lone bottle all but empty. "Where am I meant to be?"

He jumped to his feet and caught her before she fell. He picked her up and carried her through the connecting door and laid her on the big bed. Like Sleeping Beauty, her dark hair feathered across the pale pillow sham. Her breath exuded the smell of vintage grapes. The sheen of her last sip still glistened on her lips; her breathing looked heavy and even. He bent over her and kissed her.

Steps clomped somewhere down the hall followed by a high-pitched voice and the sound of a door slamming shut. He walked over and shut his, or more correctly, Tori's door.

"I'm as bad as Wheems," he muttered. Heading for his room he paused at the end of her bed and picked up the costume Bertie had left the previous day. It looked even less appealing.

Certain Tori was in a drunken comatose state, he stripped down to his briefs and pulled on the brown trousers, which were too snug for his liking. He dismissed the idea of wearing the thing Bertie had called a dickey front. In Kale's opinion, a man shouldn't wear just a collar and a bit of shirt. He would wear one of his own, a Sea Island broadcloth with spiked collar.

The black vest, embroidered with gold down the front, was a size too small, but would do if he didn't have to lift anything. The boots fit like gloves.

"What a man," slurred Tori, her head propped on one elbow. "Did you know Loretta Snow almost made it as movie star? She starred in a few minor films and then went and married Abner. Chucked it all away for love, she did."

Kale shrugged to hide his embarrassment and chided himself silently for not suspecting a possum. "Clothes are too tight," he said.

"But Bertie bought it just for you, new," she said, "except for the jacket."

He slipped on the jacket. "Yuck. It smells of mothballs." From one pocket, he withdrew the offending mothballs, and from the other, a note. Dropping the mothballs out an open window, he quickly unfolded the note and read:

Meet me in the top passage at midnight. Twenty paces, five stones down, two across, right side.

Chapter Eight

Kale lingered over the meaning of the note a moment, then quickly shoved it back into his pocket. Tori had been shaken enough. He would find the passage and be at the appointed time and place, alone.

Guests arrived in droves through the whole afternoon. Downstairs, by the reception, Bertie's packed taproom reeked of expensive perfume and cigars with a bottom note of naphthalene from the mothball-ridden costumes.

"It's the free beer room at a Dickens convention," he whispered into Tori's wimple hat and gave her a push into the seventeenth century.

Tori held her head high and swished into the room like a high-fashion model, effectively pulling the plug on the buzz of conversation. Her turn on the costume catwalk earned a huge round of applause that she acknowledged with a curtsey and a cute tilt of her wimple-clad head.

Kale caught the barman's attention and ordered a double whiskey and, with much misgiving, a bottle of Moet Chandon with two straws for his partner, who a few minutes later came along smiling and breathless, with the bounteous Loretta Snow in tow. The former Hollywood hopeful wore a low-cut, green satin Marie Antoinette–style number that left little to the imagination. Kale watched the pair share bubbly straws like old friends at the oasis.

Loretta poked her finger at Tori's black habit and said, "That getup's a million on you, honey. I love the silver chain, but what's the whistle for?"

"It's a pitch pipe, a musical whistle. It came with the outfit," Tori replied, and then explained how it was used by Prioress Mary Gant to call members of her flock. "Each one of her girls had a particular tone. When she wanted to see one for any reason, she whistled her up."

"Oh, how exciting. Do give us a demonstration."

Tori happily obliged with a note in the key of C and caused the slightly tipsy Loretta to strike a provocative pose and purr, "I'm here, boss." Loretta laughed, and taking a step back caught the hem of her dress with a heel. Still laughing, she tumbled into Kale's arms.

Tori, now in stitches, blew another C note on her whistle. "Come on, Loretta, let's go talk to Uncle Bertie."

Red-faced, feeling slightly embarrassed, Kale ordered another double scotch and scanned the crowd while awaiting its delivery. Across the room, way at the back, he spotted a serious bespectacled man wearing a lime green cutaway with big brass buttons. Drink in hand, he walked across to introduce himself. The man's name was Sharton, an architect. Kale listened attentively to his dissertation on the importance of historical settings to scholars of medieval architecture. Sharton offered the Priory as an example of how social conflict and the lowly garden mole had set the parameters of fourteenth-century construction; hidey-holes, escape tunnels, and hidden substructures were the order of the day for all medieval masons and architects. "And that goes back a long way." The little man explained that he had once been paid to electronically probe the Priory. "Scads of anomalies in this building, but all I could find was one hidey-hole, and it went nowhere."

Kale, still curious about how Mary Gant had conducted business, inquired about the possibility of a tunnel connecting the Priory with the church across the road.

"Not a chance. That idea was completely explored by a geologist. Retired chap named Cassidy. He liked to come here and muck about in the old slate quarries for fossils and other such rubbish. Nice enough chap. I got to know him quite well, but he disappeared off the face of the earth about six months ago. I heard the police started inquiries but gave up. His girlfriend said he'd run off to Fiji." Sharton laughed. He further explained that the geologist's efforts had been in vain. "All the substrata hereabouts are especially hard slate. You can see it piled around everywhere. Stuff's hard as iron; hit it with a hammer and it rings like a bell. No, a tunnel would be a most difficult undertaking, even for experienced miners using explosives." Kale nodded, more convinced than ever that Mary Gant had used the underground stream. But that knowledge didn't bring him any closer to the whereabouts of the diamond.

A gong sounded, and gentlemen began offering their arms to the ladies. He found Tori still gabbing with Loretta and offered her a crooked arm. The gong sounded again, and without a word being spoken, the entire group paraded into the dining hall and circled once around the huge table with Lord Bertie acting as Grand Marshall.

"Quaint custom," Kale whispered.

"It's not quaint. Lots of people do this on high holidays."

Kale thought the changes in the dining room were a pleasant surprise. The horseshoe-seating diagram in the booklet was there; also crisp linen, glistening crystal, and great baskets of fresh roses. In the center of the horseshoe sat the great pontificating chair. On its orange-colored canopy were the words *Liberty or Beef,* just like the original in Bertie's booklet. Kale wondered if it was the original chair. It had to be.

Bertie seated his guests like a ringmaster. While still on his feet, he introduced forty odd from memory, told one unfunny joke and passed the floor to Mary Gant, aka Tori Roche.

Tori took her place on the pontificating chair and gave a short, very informative speech on roses. Surprised by her knowledge of horticulture Kale sat enthralled, and wondering where she'd found the time to put it together. Harry had brought roses for her desk every other week for two years, but Kale had no idea she had such a thorough knowledge of them. Harry had always brought Neddy a bouquet as well. Kale was thinking of Harry when the fellow sitting next to him was called to the chair.

Kale's breathing turned difficult—he was next. A dribble of cold sweat ran down his side. He hated giving speeches and was totally unprepared. He swallowed his pride and beckoned to Sharton the architect who sat two down on his left. "Why the speeches? Do we have to give one?" he whispered.

"Part of the game. It was in the booklet, right after the Rummoli rules. Just give a spiel on anything you like."

In a panic, Kale frantically searched his pockets for Bertie's booklet, but found only mothballs and the note.

Bertie called Lord Alexander Caddington twice and would still be calling if Tori hadn't shot an elbow into his ribs. Caddington was his character, what could he talk about? Kale's short speech on bookbinding went over like a big yawn, but his jokes got plenty of laughs, and when he returned to his seat Tori squeezed his hand, which made it all worthwhile.

The wine flowed and the roasts were carved and served up with five kinds of vegetables and a pudding, and then the stories from the chair began again in earnest.

Kale considered the idea of the pontificating chair brilliant. The predinner speeches had rid everyone of their jitters, so the pontification stories came easier. In fact, the stories became so entertaining he forgot to ask Sharton if a third brick from the top struck a chord. Instead, he showed the note to Tori.

"It smells like mothballs. What does it mean?"

"How should I know? I found it in my jacket pocket."

Tori looked again at the note, her expression turning thoughtful for a moment, then she shrugged and tucked the paper into the deepest pocket of her habit.

"Hey, give me that!"

"I'll scream."

Like a referee, Bertie stood and tapped his glass with a silver spoon. "If I can have your cooperation for a few minutes, we'll clear space and begin our after-dinner rummoli game."

Away went the flowers, the crystal, the linen, and in rolled a huge round playing board about two heads taller than Kale. Kale had never thought of the simple rummoli boardgame being played on such a grand scale. With a goodly amount of help from the guests, the giant board was soon wrestled up onto the horseshoe of tables, and the game got underway.

Sixteen painted on pay-windows rimmed the huge round board. Neatly painted renditions of ancient cards headed up every window except the seven, eight, and nine, in one suit and the poker-pot window. In the center was a large, round rummoli window, the jackpot, and Kale remembered it could really pile up the loot.

Bertie snapped open a half-dozen packs of playing cards, deposited them in a shuffling machine, and flipped the switch. As the machine whirred into action,

Bertie's serving wenches moved among the guests passing out packets of chips.

Bertie repeated the instructions and announced the grand payoff. "The first player to get rid of all his cards wins the rummoli pot. You'll also have a go at finding a quarter share of a hidden treasure." In the sudden buzz of excited conversation, Bertie held aloft an artist's rendering of Prioress Mary's egg-sized diamond.

Tori looked at Kale and smiled. "Get two bags."

"Ladies and Gentlemen, the game has begun, please ante up," Bertie called as the shuffling machine began shooting out two hands per player.

The first move was Bertie's decision to play his hand and auction his extra, unseen widow hand to the highest bidder, or to play the widow and discard his first hand.

"The hand is for auction," Bertie called, and held the widow hand up for grabs. One minute of furious bidding and it was gone to an older, very attractive woman sitting next to Abner Snow. She won the Rummoli and ran off toward the secret door by the kitchen. Meanwhile, Kale was ahead by several hundred pounds.

The hours passed quickly. Kale doubled his original thousand pounds. Every woman at the table had run off to the kitchen to search for the long missing diamond. All the chairs had been cleared away and Kale found himself standing beside an excited Abner Snow—a losing Abner Snow—who told Kale he didn't really care about the treasure hunt and the legend of the diamond. He'd found a new game to showcase in his four London gaming clubs that would amount to more than any treasure hunt. After a bit of gaming banter, Kale decided he liked Abner Snow in spite of Harry's hatred of the man. But when Kale inquired after Abner's clubs, Mr. Hollywood told him in a charming manner to bugger off and mind his own business.

Kale won the next Rummoli and gave Abner a big smile as he raked in his winnings. Still smiling, he walked into the kitchen, picked up a torch from a box that had a "bring me back" sign posted over it, and taking a deep breath, headed up the narrow back staircase. He ran into Tori on the third landing; she looked all wide-eyed and breathless.

"I've found something, a very bad something," she whispered. Only before she could elaborate, a blood-curdling scream echoed from the innards of the Priory.

"What was that?"

"I shouldn't have left it open." Grabbing up her skirts, Tori turned and bolted through a thin slit in the wall.

Kale followed into a maze filled with fleeing, panic-stricken women in flounce costumes. A few seconds later, somewhere in the middle of the crisscross of passages, Kale saw Tori stop before an open section of wall and bite her knuckles. Coming up behind, he looked over her shoulder into a small room that housed a very thirsty-looking corpse.

Chapter Nine

Bertie arrived on the scene red-faced and puffing hard. He held a handkerchief to his nose while he leaned in to examine the dead man's shriveled face. "That's Edward Cassidy, the mining engineer. I thought he was in Fiji."

Harry came next. He looked down at the desiccated corpse, glanced around the little room, and shook his head. "It's been in here for months. Very interesting, look how the fingernails are shredded; like it clawed at the stone."

Tori blanched. "*It* has a name, Harry: Edward Cassidy."

Her disapproval stated, she added, "I have to get out of here, it smells awful." The ancient, six-by-eight-foot hidey-hole was rank with decay. Tori, overwrought at having found the corpse and unable to stand the smell, slipped the mothball note back to Kale. "I'll be in my room," she said, and retreated down the passage.

Kale toyed with the scrap of a paper in his pocket and felt overwhelmed by the thought that he was supposed to find Cassidy's remains.

He wasn't ready to tell anyone about the note. It might implicate him somehow. But Harry had been right; someone else had to know of the room's existence. Perhaps that architect, Sharton. He turned to Bertie, "I'm guessing this room isn't on your map."

Bertie shook his head. "It will be now. Rather looks like I'll have to call it the Cassidy room."

The irony would have made Kale laugh if the matter weren't so serious. Poor Cassidy had trekked a tough road to posterity.

The dour-faced receptionist, Jenkins, who looked as if this entire business was just a daily occurrence, arrived at the head of three Oddington police constables.

"Oddington is closer than Bourton," Bertie whispered, "but Scotland Yard will be here soon."

Bertie took Jenkins gently by the shoulder and steered her away from the doorway. "Go back downstairs," he said, "there's been a tragic accident."

"That be no accident," Jenkins replied. "That be foul murder. He oughtn't to have been poking around."

Jenkins pushed her way through the crowd of curious guests and strode off into the darkness.

Kale looked away from the departing Jenkins down to the late Mr. Cassidy. What did she mean, poking around? Had she known Cassidy was searching the passages?

Sharton had been convinced the tunnel search had been abandoned. Bertie was the one pushing for the passages to be searched. Certainly, Bertie wouldn't have killed Cassidy. Bertie was no murderer, was he? He looked around at Bertie and immediately dismissed the idea.

Kale moved beside the constables at the doorway and watched Harry poke about in the little room as if he were Sherlock Holmes. Harry examined the corpse thoroughly, then stood up, lit his cigar, and puffed out a great cloud of tobacco smoke.

Kale let out a groan. "The air is bad enough already."

Harry began to examine the wall next to the door. Kale leaned in through the doorway to observe.

"Look here constables!" Harry called, puffing his cigar. A penknife appeared in his hand and he dug about between the stones for a few minutes. "Here is the instrument of poor Mister Cassidy's demise."

Kale felt like a squeezed lemon as the doorway suddenly filled with constables. "You see this?" Harry waved a piece of wire under their noses. "It opened the door from the inside. At least it did until somebody cut it. If you don't know to keep the door propped open, it's a death trap."

"Bloody right, too," murmured one constable, scratching his head.

"Everybody out," ordered the constable in charge. "I'm declaring this a crime scene. We don't want to muck it up for Scotland Yard."

Outside in the passage away from the constables, Bertie's stiff demeanor told what he thought of Harry's conclusions.

"You deduced a murder? How?"

Harry took his time responding and puffed out another huge cloud of cigar smoke. "There is no other explanation for it. That room was meant to guard something—set up like a mousetrap."

Kale was impressed.

Harry made a hammering motion, "Mister Cassidy struck the cheese, and snap, he died a very gruesome death. Did you see the matches scattered on the floor? He must have used them very sparingly, but most are in one corner. He found something there and needed light."

"What do you think it was?"

"Dunno, but I'm going to find out. Kale, I want you to go back and tell those constables that Lord Bertillon wants to see them all immediately." Turning to Bertie, he said, "Keep them busy for thirty seconds. I want another peek at that room."

Kale didn't like it and went back grumbling that Harry was going to get them all slung into jail. "Lord Bertillon wants to see you fellows," he told the Oddington constabulary and was more than a little surprised at how rapidly they acquiesced. The smell he figured, and he turned to follow them, gagging at the stench.

"Kale, stay here, keep guard," Harry whispered, passing by quickly.

Cigar smoke billowing from the door of the little room made Kale nauseous, but it masked the odor of death. "Harry? Do you really think somebody locked Cassidy in this room?"

"Yes, and they wanted to make it look like an accident," Harry whispered from inside the room. Another few seconds and he trotted out smiling. "There's little hard evidence that it's not an accident. That device may have been cut decades ago. The coroner will likely call it death by misadventure and that will be the end of it. Scotland Yard will come and root about and then lose interest. It was a very good method to do away with someone."

Kale nodded in agreement and thought again of that receptionist Jenkins. She had been awfully sure of murder. He suddenly thought it very odd that apart from Jenkins, not a single staff member had come to gawk at the corpse in the little room. "Harry, what was Cassidy using all those matches for? What did you find?"

"Empty bottles."

"Bottles?"

"No time to explain; I have to see a man about a horse."

Five burley men from Scotland Yard clomped up the back stairs making noise like a whole soccer team. Two began investigating the crime scene, taping off the area, taking pictures. The others herded curious onlookers down to the dining room. Kale and Bertie ducked through a secret fireplace door into a nearby suite.

A muscular, heavyset inspector found them pondering the situation. "Lord Bertillon, would you be good enough to assemble your remaining guests? We've a few questions to put to them."

Bertie nodded. "Right, of course I will."

Kale followed Bertie and the inspector into the hallway but changed direction and headed for Tori's suite.

He found her stretched out on her bed staring glassy-eyed at the ceiling. He sat down beside her and caressed her arm.

"Are you okay?"

"Kale, that poor man died such a horrible death, alone in the dark. How horrible."

"I know, I know."

"This isn't just some folklore to be guessed at anymore. It's more than a treasure hunt game. I don't think I considered it real before now. That poor man was looking for the diamond. It killed him."

"Harry said somebody booby-trapped the door. Listen now, the police want to question everyone. You're the one who found him. We need to go down and tell them what happened."

"He was murdered. What can I tell them about that? I simply followed the directions in your note. I opened the door, and there he was. I haven't anything else to say."

"They'll think of some questions. You just answer what you know and leave the conclusions to them. I recommend you not voluntarily mention the note."

Tori rolled onto her side and looked at him. "What does Harry say?"

He glanced over at the fireplace and back to Tori's pale, troubled face. He wondered if she could handle the questioning. "Harry says for you to keep your wits about you, and don't volunteer any information."

A knock sounded at the door. "Jenkins here, miss. The inspectors need you downstairs for questioning."

Kale escorted Tori downstairs and they were directed to a table in the deserted taproom. The inquisitor, a tall, thin, dapper looking man bustled through the door. He introduced himself as Chief Inspector Jeremy Slagin and pointed a finger at Tori. Before he could utter a word, Harry sauntered through the door and sat two tables away puffing his cigar. The Chief Inspector threw a chilly look at Harry. Kale watched a palpable undercurrent of resentment course between the two before the inspector turned back to Tori.

"Miss Roche, I've been assigned to investigate the death of Mister . . ." He glanced down at his file, "Mister Edward Cassidy, late of Swindon Town. I only have a few questions."

"I'll help anyway I can, Inspector."

"Fine. Now, did you know the deceased man? Had you ever met him before?"

"No. Never."

"How did you happen upon that room Miss Roche? It was very well concealed."

Kale held his breath. The inspector continued before Tori could respond.

"Were you just walking along indiscriminately pushing stones looking for a secret door?"

Kale breathed easier. The inspector liked to answer his own questions.

"That's exactly what I was doing. You understand it was a treasure hunt. Unfortunately, I happened to find a secret room."

"Yes, Lord Bertillon has already explained his little treasure hunt."

Chief Inspector Slagin's few questions became ever more detailed, first directed at Tori and then at Kale, and went on for twenty minutes. Then, seemingly satisfied, the chief inspector declared the interview over. Kale took Tori by the hand, and, exhausted, the two climbed the stairs to their rooms.

The next morning at first light, the repeated clanking of stone from outside awoke Kale and caused him to stumble from his bed to the window, ready to shout obscenities at Hermes Wheems.

But it wasn't Wheems. Instead, there was Harry, wearing shorts and a baggy gray sweatshirt, busily pulling stones from the low wall fronting the church grounds. Kale watched him pile the large flat stones into what was shaping up to be a neat pyramid. He'd heard Tori's description of Harry's wall-building exercise regime, but had never actually seen it performed. He imagined Harry back at his farm in Ireland doing the task in a brown suit. Tori had said the regime was simple; he just moved a pyramid of boulders from one side of his front door to the other, and he did that every single morning. Kale chuckled, leaned on the sill, and watched a few moments longer before deciding to go down and join him.

In ten minutes, Kale had showered, dressed, and descended to the parking lot where he noticed only a few of the guests' cars remained. Bertie's weekend treasure hunt had gone bust. Murder had that effect on parties.

Harry had a goodly portion of the stone wall dismantled and stacked into a perfect five-foot pyramid and was now busily digging into the hard exposed earth with a spade. "No mortar," he said not looking up. "A bit sloppy on their part not to make it harder to dismantle."

Kale, who was sure most rock walls in England were stacked without mortar, shrugged, selected a suitable part of the pyramid, and sat down. "Harry, what are you expecting to find here? Please tell me you're not looking for that stupid diamond. There's another fifty feet of wall; it's a needle in a haystack."

Harry said nothing and continued shoveling dirt from the hole. Kale shrugged and bent down to examine the dirt. He noticed tiny bits of white stuff in the soil.

"Give me the note, Kale."

Kale blanched. He didn't think anyone other then Tori knew about that note, and she'd promised not to tell anyone. "What?"

Harry stopped digging and wiped the sweat from his brow. "The note you found in your pocket, give it here." He leaned on his shovel and looked up. "I wrote that note. I wrote in the coordinates and put Cassidy's coat back with the other costumes. I'd no idea you'd be wearing the thing. I only wanted someone to find Cassidy's body. It couldn't be me, you understand?"

Kale did not understand. He stood and shifted nervously from one foot to the other, looking about, thinking hard. If Harry had found the hidey-hole and its grizzly contents before Tori, then maybe Bertie knew Cassidy had been missing.

Something clicked. Bertie had to know. He'd found

the coat back in with the costumes. Kale now understood why the rest of his costume had been bought new. But, if Bertie had shut Cassidy in that room, wouldn't he have remembered leaving him fully dressed? And wouldn't he have searched the coat pockets when he found it returned? Questions flew through Kale's mind, paralyzing his trust in anyone.

Harry hoisted another shovelful from his deepening hole and stopped. He looked up, and Kale knew mistrust must be written on his face.

"I found the body yesterday morning, Kale. I found it before I came into Tori's room through that secret door. That messenger from London? He brought me a high-tech ultraviolet scanner. I was up in that maze of passages looking for the diamond when I found footsteps in the dust. I followed them, that's all."

Kale said nothing.

"Kale, don't you understand the value of that stone? Whoever finds it will be fixed for life. And we need fixing."

"Did you find it?"

"No. And I didn't want to be the one who found Cassidy's body. I thought if he were found during the party, it might spring a reaction, some clue to his death."

After a deadlock of eyes, Harry turned away and thrust the shovel into the hole and hit something hard. Kale leaned forward, expecting to see metal, but nothing was visible. Harry took the shovel to the hole a bit more gently, and after clearing the dirt from around whatever had made the noise, he pried the object into view.

Kale shuddered. "It's a skull."

Harry hoisted his gruesome prize into the pale morning light and began dusting it off. "The skull of a small woman, with perfect teeth. Kale, meet one of Mary's pretty maids in a row." Harry scuffled into the hole with the toe of his shoe and, ducking down, came up with two more grizzly prizes.

"Yuck!"

Harry dusted off the bulbous remains, laid them down beside the hole, and picked up the spade. In less than an hour he'd unearthed an even dozen and had them lined up beside his trench like a macabre necklace. He dug for another few feet and gave up. No number thirteen; no Mary Gant. Just twelve pretty maids in a row. "The rhyme was meant for Mary's eyes. Tori will be devastated."

"Harry, how did you know they were here?"

"A lucky guess. For ages, people have been trying to piece the murder together from clues in the rhyme. I don't know why no one thought of it before now. Or maybe they were afraid to look. Lots of superstitions in those days, right? And no one here cares about the murders. They only want the treasure. Those bits of white in the soil are cockleshells, like in the rhyme. I noticed them here last evening. You will observe that they are only here, in this one spot."

"Lime, from cockleshells!"

Harry nodded and continued, "It didn't hit me until the middle of the night. I couldn't wait for daylight to arrive."

"Look around for a whistle."

"No whistle. There's nothing more. There's no Mary

Gant." He placed the skulls back into the trench as if he was planting corn. Then he took his spade and covered them up with dirt. "Rest in peace, ladies."

Kale helped to rebuild the wall, and after moving a few stones, he stopped and looked at Harry. "How are we going to tell Tori?"

Harry heaved a stone onto the wall. "We're not. This is already too real for her to deal with. Maybe later, after the situation is sorted out."

"Which situation—the murder of those twelve ladies, or Cassidy's more recent misadventure?"

"Actually, that bit of trouble with Galley Press. They wanted the contents of that safe very badly. I do believe they won't stop looking until they find them."

Kale looked flabbergasted. "That box of papers? You mean some bozo burned the building down for those silly recipes?"

"Last night, that London messenger left behind three items I didn't tell you about. Three bozos from MI5. Bertie should lock that front door at night."

"Harry!"

"Right, the bozos. They wanted the papers from the safe, said they would use force to get it. That's what I was doing in Tori's room. I told them I'd get the box and bring it down. I'd planned to give them the slip, but on the way I saw Hermes Wheems leaving Tori's room. He was looking for the box too, but for other masters. I had to go back and get the bozos to scare Wheems off. While they were doing that, I showed the box to you and Tori."

Kale nodded his understanding, pursed his lips, and

gave a little whistle of admiration. "Are they going to keep the box?"

No. They said they only wanted to check its contents and that you would get the papers back in due time. Perhaps not every one of them, but most," he said.

Kale wondered if the one they wanted was the one Harry had told him to stash away. He stood and watched Harry shove a few smaller stones into place.

"Who were these bozos working for?"

"My money's on Abner Snow."

"You blame everything on him."

"With good reason. He's a greedy mongrel."

"I suppose you're going to tell me that Wheems works for him."

"Now isn't that an interesting thought? Maybe the connection is right under our noses." Harry stopped and frowned. "I'm beginning to think that diamond will never be recovered. I was sure somewhere in those upper passages I would find a stairway leading down to a tunnel from the Priory to the church. I was positive there was one, and that in there we would find the diamond, or at the very least a clue to its whereabouts. But even with all that high-tech gear all I could find was Cassidy's corpse."

"They are joined, Harry, by an underground stream." Kale hadn't meant to tell Harry his findings until later, but he couldn't resist and now it was too late to take back his words. He explained hearing the rushing water in the church cellar and the puff of air coming through the brazier. It felt good to be one up on the famous detective.

Harry set the last stone in place, propped the shovel by the walk, and waved toward the church.

The front door of the church was locked tight as a drum, but Harry pulled a set of picks from his pocket and after several minutes, it swung open.

Kale led the way through the door to the left of the vestibule and down the staircase to the dimly lit basement. He shoved crates from their path and pointed to the spot where he heard the running water. Harry bent to listen with his ear directly on the cold slate.

"Yes! I believe you're onto something, Kale."

"Yeah, but how are we going to get down there? Even if we do, I think all we'll find is how Mary Gant shipped her liquor. I don't think it'll lead us to any diamond. If there is a diamond."

"All roads lead to that diamond, Kale. If it's still around, we'll find it, and solve those old murders in the process."

"And hopefully not get caught in a death-trap like Cassidy," Kale added.

Chapter Ten

Kale returned to the breakfast sideboard for a third helping of Scottish kippers. One of Bertie's girls burst from the kitchen with a steaming basket of currant buns. Jenkins. She looked up and smiled. "Bun?"

"Yes, thank you very much. Tell me, Miss Jenkins, up in the passage you said something about how people shouldn't be poking around in other people's business. What did you mean?"

"Mr. Cassidy found what he was looking for, Mr. Kale. He dared to try and solve a riddle and old Lord Caddington killed him for his trouble."

"A riddle?"

"That's right. Children use it as a jump rope ditty. Well, they did when children was around here. It goes like this:

Two over, five down, pass the spirit all around.
In a wall with the mice, a private room for your

104

advice. Down a tunnel with a key, many bottles filled for thee. Shut the door, make no sound, spend your life underground. Drink, drink, change your mind. How many bottles did you find?

That rhyme's as old as the village, a warning from Lord Caddington to stay out of his cellars. Every child knows that. But we never could figure out what it meant. Mister Cassidy figured out the real meaning— five stones down. We use to look, you know. All us kids looked everywhere. That Lord Caddington, he went crazy, died in a fire in that manor soon after the nuns were murdered. The town died too. And the manor sat empty for ages until Lord Bertillon's family laid claim to it through lineage from Lady Caddington's second marriage." She looked to her tray. "Lovely buns, hot from the oven."

Kale nibbled a bun and mulled over the rhyme. The whole place is one big mystery. He looked around and saw Tori gathering her things for a move. She motioned toward another table beside a front window. One glance out that window and Kale understood; a bus filled with workmen had just arrived across the road at Mary's church.

Kale returned with his hot kippers and elected to stand at the window. He forked up morsels of the tender smoky delights and watched the cadre of workers fan out toward their appointed tasks.

Moments later Harry slid into the seat opposite Tori. He stared out the window and began picking at the label from a jam jar.

Kale stiffened and spat a small bone onto his plate. Did Harry have to constantly slide in between them? He might be a great detective, but he couldn't seem to pick up on the signs that he was horning in on another guy's territory. Or maybe he did. Kale turned back to watch the workers across the road scurrying onto the roof like ants and reminded himself five times that Harry was not competition. He spoke without looking away from the workers across the road. "Harry, try the fresh currant buns with your marmalade."

"Right! I believe I will."

Tori chuckled and reached for the jam jar. "Harry, you've worried the label off two jars already."

As if reminded there were better pursuits than picking labels, Harry smiled and headed off for the sideboard.

"He's very upset about something," Tori whispered.

Kale glanced toward the sideboard and nodded. Harry looked worn out.

Tori, on the other hand, looked very refreshed, all healthy, glowing pink and lovely in a skimpy designer dress. He liked the way she had her hair pulled back and tied with a ribbon.

"Kale! You're wool-gathering."

"Sorry. What did you say?"

"I said, Harry is worried about something—look what he's done to the marmalade jar. He picked the labels at the other table as well."

Kale turned half around and looked across the empty room to the sideboard where their squat friend stood munching a bun and talking to Jenkins. "Yeah, well, I think for the first time in his career he's baffled. I think it bothers him not to be able to put his finger on what's going on here."

"What is going on here?"

"Who knows? But something is. Across the road I give you exhibit A. Abner Snow already has four successful gambling clubs. Why would he want to open another, and in the middle of nowhere?"

"Do you think Abner knows about the water under the church?"

"I would consider it a distinct possibility. It shouldn't take a genius to figure out what runs that big fruit press. Abner is like a rat smelling cheese."

"Look! Do you see what they're pulling off the bus? It's a compressor. They use it to power jackhammers. There! There's the hammer. He'll be pounding through the slate floor before long. We'd better think of something quickly."

At midmorning, the trio was still in the dining hall nibbling currant buns when the huge lorry pulled to a stop across the road. Harry left the table and nonchalantly strolled out the door and across the road for a peek inside the truck. He returned a few minutes later to report it contained all the odds and ends needed to open a gaming establishment. "He's got a big electric sign in that truck. He's calling the place 'Black Mary's'."

Tori looked outraged and demanded they march over for an explanation. "I'm not going to have my relative maligned in such a tawdry fashion. Let's go!"

She was out the door before Kale could stop her, running down the driveway with both arms flailing. Without stopping to check for traffic, she dashed across the road and was nearly run over by Chief Inspector Slagin.

"There's trouble," Harry said. "One thing we do not need at this juncture is for Slagin to come poking around. He'll run us all out of here and we'll never get to the bottom of this mystery."

"Harry, did you tell Tori about finding the skulls?"

"No, and I'm not going to. I'll leave that for you. Why?"

"I don't know; she's getting really protective about that church."

He saw Tori lean into the open window of Slagin's car and begin talking away like they were old friends.

"I better get her away from there," Kale said, and started toward the road with long strides. Before he could reach her Tori opened the door and climbed into the car. Kale immediately turned and retraced his steps.

The two talkers finally emerged from the car with Tori still jabbering away. She gestured toward the church, grabbed Slagin by the hand, and began pulling him across the road. Kale exchanged a bemused look with Harry.

Behind them, the hotel door opened and out stepped Bertie. "Morning all. Glorious day," he said. No one responded. "What, is something wrong?"

Kale pointed to the church and Bertie's cheery demeanor fell like London Bridge. "Looks like your friend Abner Snow has bought the old church."

The three watched Tori and the chief inspector walk into the church. Harry suggested it might be a good idea for Bertie to get over there and help protect his interests. "You wouldn't want him digging the place up and making a mess without a permit."

From the depths of the church came the sound Kale had been expecting all morning, the staccato pounding of a jackhammer.

Bertie, Kale, and Harry set off toward the church at a fast clip. They wove around Abner's workers, ran into the church, and clattered down the cellar steps just as the jackhammer fell silent. Tori stood in front of Abner Snow wagging her finger and declaring with a stern face and shaky voice that she would stand guard to prevent any further degradation of this culturally important edifice. "Chief Inspector Slagin has deemed this building an important cultural heritage. We'll let the courts deal with the issue."

Abner Snow looked as if he would suffer a conniption. Chief Inspector Slagin stood beside the two looking amused until he spotted Harry. The Chief Inspector came across dodging puddles almost at a run, his animosity flying like a flag.

"Bass, I demand to know what you are doing here. I tolerated your presence at the crime scene last night because of your involvement, but I don't jolly well think you can step in wherever you please. This is Yard business. It doesn't concern you."

Harry shrugged. "I was buying a horse hereabouts and saw the excitement going on. This church is a real beauty, Jeremy. Is the lass right? Can you declare it a tentative historical sight for her?"

"You know I can't. And I don't think Abner Snow will pay much attention to my cease and desist order. In a few hours he'll be back working." Slagin took Harry off into a corner for a palaver. Left alone, Kale surveyed Abner's motley crew of workers. Thugs, only thugs. He locked eyes with Hermes Wheems. The giant stood next to the fruit press, leaning on it, staring at him. *So that's how it is.*

Bertie began shooing workers from the church. Harry and the chief inspector walked behind, Slagin pausing to say good-bye to Tori and tell her he'd warned Abner Snow not to dig on pain of arrest. He allowed Kale a nod.

Harry returned to Kale's side with news. "Our dear Chief Inspector has little interest in pursuing Mr. Cassidy's death, and he had the absolute gall to ask me to keep an eye on Abner Snow. He says there's just enough suspicion to warrant attention, but not enough evidence to keep his men tied to the job."

Kale wondered what had prompted the inspector to seek help. "Harry, does the chief inspector think Abner Snow killed Cassidy?"

Harry shrugged his wide shoulders while staring pensively down at the abandoned air hammer. "Thing barely made a dent in that floor."

Kale related what the architect, Sharton, had said about the slate substrata being hard as iron. "The stream has to be natural and must flow into the Evenlode. Bertie said the Priory was originally a Norman castle. It only makes sense to build over a source of water. I'm certain Mary Gant used it to smuggle her booze." He walked in circles, then crouched and poked absentmindedly at the beginnings of a hole made by the jackhammer. Tori sat nearby on a crate recovering from her speech and temporary victory. Kale stood and whispered, "Harry, I think we'd better get down there tonight. There has to be another way in."

Harry nodded, "You're right. Time is ticking and putting us farther away from solving the nursery rhyme murders."

Tori sagged under the weight of his words. "I'd almost put that out of my mind today. I don't even want to think of those murders."

Harry patted her arm. "Come on. Let's you and I take a break from this business and have us a peek at Bertillon Manor."

"No, I'm staying here. Mary Gant did not run away. She died here. I know it with every fiber of my being. I'm going to protect her memory. They won't dig if I'm here. Kale can show you the manor."

Kale gave her a look he hoped she interpreted as admiration and followed Harry up the stairs.

In the car, driving slowly, Harry explained his motive for looking at the manor. "Bertie told me Abner Snow is making noise about buying the place."

Kale shook his head, speechless, knowing they were on a hunt. Was there a hidden link between the manor, the Priory, and the church?

Harry grunted in appreciation of the great building as they drove down to the very end of the lane, where the river edged the property line. Kale didn't bother with a question, he just followed his stubby companion through a path in the alder scrub to the grassy bank of the Evenlode River. Arms akimbo, Harry looked upstream, downstream, and then kicked at the weathered remnants of an ancient dock. He raised an arm and pointed to the middle of the river. "See that long ripple? What do you think it means? The rest is calm as glass."

Kale gazed out at the water trying to decipher the meaning of a long ripple in the middle of a calm stream. "Well, there must be something on the bottom causing turbulence."

Harry removed his shirt, pants, shoes, and dove into the water. He surfaced, squirting water from his mouth.

Rooted like a tree, Kale watched Harry swim the thirty feet to the middle and dive down. He waited. Looking around, he was struck by the beauty of the classic English river: green banks and water so clear he could see steps leading to the bottom and Harry fooling about with a length of old rusty chain.

A few minutes later, Harry swam back to shore and dripped all the way back to the car. He opened the boot, stripped off his underwear, and while still soaking wet changed into rumpled white slacks and a red Hawaiian shirt. He completed his ensemble by pulling on white loafers.

Kale laughed.

"What's wrong?"

"Nothing, I just didn't think you owned anything but brown suits and blue shirts."

Harry tossed his wet clothes into the boot and slammed it closed. He winked at Kale. "It's one of my disguises, innit?"

This time Kale roared with laughter.

Harry grinned at him good-humoredly. "I'll bet you think ministers sleep in their white collars."

In the car, Harry became serious again. "I know everything I need to know about Mary Gant, except why she was killed."

"You found all that out on the bottom of the river? What was down there?"

"A chain. A very old and very long chain." Harry gunned the Mercedes all the way up the lane and slewed sideways onto the main road.

Chapter Eleven

As they sped along in the Mercedes, the sun painted the tiny village with splashes of light and dark that reminded Kale of a Van Gogh canvas. "Are you going to tell me what you know?"

"It's obvious. Think about it."

Kale tried to piece the facts together. Twelve ladies murdered, but not Mary Gant—maybe. The Priory, the church, and the manor riddled with passageways. Is there a connection? What do those three places have in common? About to give up, he was suddenly struck by the answer. "Harry, it's the river. The Evenlode connects all the passages. Abner Snow has it figured out and wants to own all three. He's using the gambling house as a cover up."

"Told you it was obvious."

"Harry, where does that Hermes Wheems fit it? If he works for the monks, why was he helping Abner dig a hole in the slate? And what does any of it have to do with that box from Galley Press' safe?" Kale shook his head. "Mary Gant must have had something more valuable than a diamond she wore around her neck."

"She did. The recipe."

"What recipe?"

"The recipe I gave you from the metal box. It's more than a brandy recipe. You heard Tori. A single drink would send you off for the better of a week."

"But the recipes were marked with the monks' seal."

"Right! She gave it to them for safekeeping when she sensed danger. They promised to guard it. They're still doing that, only they didn't figure on Tulley stumbling across it while researching their history."

"I can't believe anyone would kill for a recipe."

"I'm told it was potent medicine. It made people loony; loony enough to kill for it. At any rate, we can't breathe a word. I promised the monks we'd give it back."

"You what?"

"Don't know about you, but I'd like to live to a ripe old age."

Harry drove slowly and by the time they reached the Priory, darkness had claimed the empty car park. "Poor Bertie. His treasure hunt's a bust."

They found Bertie rushing out from behind the reception counter, his arms loaded with boxes of wine glasses and looking anything but unhappy. Pausing only long enough to tell them Tori was in the suite changing back into her costume, he trotted into the taproom.

Kale looked confused and shouted, "Why?"

"We made the news today," Bertie called back. "Every radio and telly talk show is calling to inquire about the nursery rhyme murders and the hunt for Mary Gant's diamond. The telephone hasn't stopped ringing. The hotel is booked solid tonight." Bertie stuck his head out the doorway. "The treasure hunt party is on again, lads. Get changed, quickly now. Guests are coming!"

Harry and Kale both laughed. The place was deserted.

"Believe me, the hotel *is* booked solid," Bertie reiterated. "The people *are* coming. Now hurry."

In good humor, the men trudged up the steps to the top floor and went their separate ways to change. In the shower, watching the water flow down the drain, Kale pondered the mystery of the missing diamond and the underground stream. What if Mary had met a different fate than her twelve ladies? What if she'd been drowned in the Evenlode? Then her diamond *would* be along the streambed. They had to find a way down to that stream, and quickly. There had to be a way down, but where? They couldn't return to the church tonight. Abner would most certainly post a guard—probably that monster Hermes Wheems. No, they'd have to find another way. Looking at the drain suddenly provided an idea. In his mind's eye, Kale traced the progress of Mary's product. Fruit squeezed in the old church cellar, juice fermented, distilled, bottled and crated. Then she'd tossed the crates into that underground stream. It was the only way. But where was it distilled? At what place were the crates pulled from the Evenlode? They wouldn't ferment and distill where they pressed; the stink would have given the game away. Suddenly it all clicked. Only one place made any sense: a spot where the smell could be masked by other smells. Kale hurried through the rest of his shower, and to avoid any bickering with Bertie, he donned his foppish Lord Caddington costume.

He found Tori dressed and applying makeup in the dressing room. Gilding the lily, he thought, and leaned against the doorframe while she related how Abner's crew had turned the main floor of the church into a gambling hall. "It's not the Ritz, but it will do. Abner came down to the cellar with a bottle of champagne and the judge's order that allows him access to all space but the cellar. He's up to no good, Kale. He's onto another agenda. Did you and Harry tour the manor room by room?"

"No, we didn't go into the manor. Harry went for a swim in the river."

Tori smiled. "You're kidding."

"I wish!" Kale explained all he thought permissible including the revelation about the recipe.

Rain whipped against the big Elizabethan windows turning an already black night blacker. Something caught Kale's eye; he walked over and stared beyond the blurred dark of the parking lot and was not surprised to see the *Black Mary's Club* sign flicker and glow brightly. "No moss grows on old Abner," he muttered and turned around to see Tori seated on the bed leafing through her murdered relative's formula book. Her face looked serious in the frame of the nun's wimple, and she spoke without lifting her eyes. "I thought discovering Mary's fate would have a more uplifting effect; but somehow it makes me unhappy. Kale, we had better get down to supper before the rush."

He laughed. "You're as loopy as Bertie. There's not a sign of any headlamps on that road and the hotel is deserted. I don't know why I even bothered putting on this getup. We ought to forget the costumes and get down to the cellar."

"A cellar? Here? Bertie never mentioned the Priory having a cellar. It's not on his map."

"Yeah, well, he knows it's there. But like all the king's tax collectors, and those jump-rope kids, he can't find the way." He sat on the bed and told her about the kitchen brazier, the puffs of charcoal dust, and the hook on the ceiling. "In Mary's time they would haul up that grill and dump the spent coals down the hole, like in a fireplace. A cellar is the only place Mary could have distilled brandy without stinking up the neighborhood. Roasting meat will mask any smell."

"You think there's a door?"

"More like Alice's rabbit hole."

"Oh, how very clever of you, Kale. She probably cooked beef twenty-four hours a day. We should have thought of that. Thinking of it now makes me hungry; let's hurry down and eat. I won't be able to trek off on an adventure without a full stomach. And you're wrong about the crowd. In an hour this hotel will be jammed with people dressed in period costume ready to hunt for treasure. It was Abner that leaked the story to the media, Bertie told me. Everyone within driving distance will be here, and soon." She rose from the edge of the bed looking every inch like Prioress Mary Gant.

"Abner leaked the story? That's not good at all."

"Quite. He and Bertie have an arrangement. To-night's Rummoli game will be held across the road in Abner's new club complete with a jazz band. There'll be noise enough for him to run that hammer again."

Looking at her brought a new thought. "Tori, if William was truly Mary's son, why didn't she give him the diamond?"

"My granny told me it wasn't hers. She was holding it as collateral on a loan. Besides, I told you William died young."

"The daughter, then?"

"I don't know. She was probably something Granny dreamed up. I've a feeling the family descended from William having a teenage roll in the hay, a pastime that still seems to run in my family. Let's go. I'm famished."

Tori had been on the money about the crowds. Within the hour the dining room filled to capacity with people talking rules of rummoli and demanding more beef. The overworked brazier would take days to cool off.

Having wisely thought to dine early, the trio relin-quished their table and sought refuge in the taproom. In there, Kale told Harry about their plan to enter the river through his prophesied brazier hole. At nine o'clock sharp, Bertie announced that Abner Snow's new Black Mary's Club was open for Rummoli and gave instruc-tions that winners would need a pass to regain entrance to the hotel treasure hunt.

The trio sipped Moet Chandon and hunkered down for a long wait. They had no intention of entering Ab-ner's club.

A few minutes before midnight, the kitchen staff called it quits and headed across the road with Harry following behind, headed for his car. Bertie, too busy counting money, failed to notice the stubby ex-cop trot past him carrying a long, iron crowbar. Harry strode toward the kitchen with Tori and Kale hard on his heels.

The kitchen smelled of beef, cooking oil, and pudding. Tori opened the huge refrigerator looking for leftovers.

"Tori, forget your stomach. We've got work to do," Kale hissed.

"I'm only looking. I'm hungry."

Harry motioned her over. "Eat later."

Kale stepped up beside Harry and immediately backed away from the heat radiating from the brazier.

Tori stopped midstep. "We'll have to wait. You'll burn yourself if you touch that."

Harry grabbed some oven mitts from the sideboard.

"No," insisted Tori. "It's too hot. We'll have to cool it down." She held up a finger, walked over to the sink, and returned with a large pail of water. "If there's no time to waste and you won't let me eat, then there's nothing else for it." She stepped close and dumped the entire bucket onto the brazier. Kale laughed. Through a huge cloud of steam he saw her dash back across the kitchen and return with flashlights and oven mitts. "If there is a hole under there, I want to be first to see what's at the bottom."

Kale thought of the gruesome murders and the cellar having been locked up for centuries. "This should be as much fun as entering Hades," he muttered.

Still hot, but approachable, the trio hunkered around the brazier and on the count of three, they pushed. It slid an inch.

"Bloody heavy for cast iron," Harry said and grabbed up the long pry bar.

"Slate," Kale corrected. "Come on. Give it your all."

"Where is Wheems when we need him?" Harry said, sourly.

"Don't mention that name," Tori said. "Even with all this heat it gives me the shivers. Now grab hold, you two. Let's try harder this time. Harry, forget that iron bar and push."

Once again they hunkered down, primed their bodies, and on Harry's count of three gave a tremendous shove.

"We moved it," declared an elated Kale, "a good eight inches. And there is a hole!"

Wiping sweat from his brow Harry said, "Come on Yank, push! We need a larger hole to squeeze through."

Kale put super human effort into the next push, and the brazier slid across the floor revealing a gaping, round hole, and steps.

"Steps! Wasn't she smart to think of everything," Tori exclaimed.

Excited, Tori grabbed up a flashlight, hiked her skirts up a bit, and started down before either man could think to stop her. Harry shrugged and followed, leaving Kale to trail behind. This time he felt rather relieved to go last.

Half a dozen steps down, the heat, charcoal dust, and cobwebs gave way to cold damp air and the unmistakable sound of running water. A dozen more steps and their lamps lit up a room of gigantic proportions. Kale moved his light beam along a vaulted ceiling supported on each side by a double row of pillars. Tori played hers along rows of cobweb-festooned workbenches piled high with crates, bottles, and old corking machines. Harry's beam revealed four huge tear-shaped distilling vessels. Green from oxidation, the pot stills took up the entire end the room. With a satisfied grunt, Harry set off in that direction. Tori and Kale stepped slowly, not wanting to miss the spark of light that might prove to be the elusive diamond.

Nothing. They searched every square inch and returned to find Harry among a huge pile of sturdy oak crates. He beamed ear to ear like Alice's Cheshire cat. "Good as any diamond," he said, and passed across an opened bottle. "Mary's stuff! Raspberry brandy, 100 proof, and nothing like you've ever tasted. Not too sweet, has a real kick, and still tastes like fresh juicy raspberries. It's not her secret recipe—but it's fantastic."

Kale could read the concern in Tori's eyes.

Harry dismissed it. "Not to worry. There's nothing of Mary's girls in there. That was all done across the road. The bottling was done here."

Tori took a tiny sip of her ancestor's wares. Two more hearty sips and she passed it over to Kale pronouncing it truly wonderful and suggested they take inventory.

"Ninety-two," declared Harry, his voice coming from the dark at the back of the pile of mostly empty crates. Kale cast his beam around but Harry had disappeared from view.

"Where are you?"

"In here, partners."

Kale flashed his light and maneuvered around the crates toward the voice. Tori followed close behind. Near the back corner of the immense cellar, they found a small open doorway. Inside they found Harry and a room filled to the ceiling with cases of Mary's brandy. Wet, stale air, but quiet and not echoing with the sound of rushing water.

Harry held up an opened bottle. "Peach! And good enough to die for."

Kale winced. Many had died, and the person likely responsible for the most recent death was probably boring a hole in the church floor this very moment.

"Harry, we have to do something and quickly. Abner will get down here before long. You know he's running that Rummoli game for a reason. With nobody watching he'll be back pounding that slate and nobody will hear a thing."

Tori glared at him. "Are you suggesting I should have sat in there all night?"

"No. He would have gotten rid of you, somehow."

"Abner wouldn't hurt me."

"I didn't say that, did I?" Kale gave up his argument.

Harry suddenly upped and left the room, his head cocked, listening.

"What is it?" Kale asked stepping out behind him.

"Let's go find that underground stream."

"Wait for me," Tori wailed.

Outside the brandy room, the sound of rushing water filled the entire space, which made pinpointing its source difficult. Kale pointed to the middle of the cellar space. "It's loudest from there, I think."

Midway was a heavy oak cap with brass handles. Pulled aside it revealed a crate-sized hole in the slate floor. Their lights fell on a narrow expanse of black, rushing water—powerful water. Kale could feel the vibrations through his feet. "Stay back; it might not be safe."

"No one would be foolhardy enough to fall into that."

Tori stepped around Kale and edged closer to the opening. "Quite. It looks very cold and uninviting."

Suddenly, with a sound like a gunshot, the brittle slate under Tori's feet gave way and she dropped from sight into the fast-moving water.

Harry grabbed Kale's arm. "Go after her, but don't make too much noise," he said, and pushed him in.

Kale landed in water so cold he couldn't catch his breath. Desperately trying to get his feet under him he struck upon something he ascertained to be a metal box. Then the current shot him downstream like a bullet.

Bobbing along in the dark, Kale snatched at the rough rock walls, but to no avail. Seconds later he spotted a dim light ahead. Tori hung from what could only be the drive shaft from the fruit press. His spirits soared; what a gal. He saw her turn and put a finger across her lips to signify quiet. Grabbing for the shaft he cracked a knee on the submerged iron blades of the shaft and bit his lip to keep from crying out. Through the pain and the sound of rushing water, Kale could both hear and feel the unmistakable rapid thud of a jackhammer—Abner at work. In the light that filtered down through a dozen cracks in the ceiling, he saw a two-foot ledge and the five rusted rungs of a ladder. "It must come out beside the press. Come on, let's climb up," he whispered.

"Not with him up there." Tori strung together a blue streak of swear words and peeled off her soggy Mary Gant costume. Kale stared at her, riveted at the sight. He turned away to watch the habit float off into the dark.

"I couldn't swim with that on, but now I'm freezing in this camisole. Let's hurry and find where this ends."

Kale rolled his eyes and went zooming off after her feeling like a flushed rat.

The end came surprisingly quickly. In less than a minute the duo were spewed out a hole in a cliffside and dropped fifteen feet into calmer, warmer water. Kale reached Tori in two strokes.

Squirting water from her mouth, she pointed to the shore, but before they could move, two crates tumbled from the hole striking the water with a mighty smack.

Treading water, Tori snatched at the crate and heaved herself half onto it. "There's a note attached to this one. It's from Harry," she exclaimed, and after a bit of jockeying in the moonlight, she read it aloud: *Hang on. Bertie helping. Meet you at the Manor.*

Kale grabbed hold of the second crate and heard Tori whisper, "Are we traveling to Bertillon Manor on these crates? How can they float after two hundred years?"

"Hearts of oak, built well, and waterproofed with paraffin. I'll bet they even dovetailed the edges. Remember, I told you Harry went for a swim? Well, he found a chain at the bottom of the river and now I know what it was for: Lord Caddinton had a system rigged to catch these crates. He must have been in on Mary's scheme."

Tori shivered. "I can't believe Harry expects us to hang onto these crates all the way to the manor. I'm going to freeze my butt."

"Keep it up out of the water. Really, the air is warmer, but it shouldn't take long; no more than a half hour, and it's better than walking. Much better for you."

She grinned. Her ready reply was cut short as more crates splashed down from the hole in the cliffside. "Come on, it's not safe here." With a few forceful kicks, they propelled the crates further from the shore into the briskly moving current.

"Kale, you lead the way."

Kale's guesstimate proved correct. In less than a half hour they found Harry and Bertie waiting by the river-bank at Bertillon Manor. Pressure lanterns lit up the area like Coney Island but made finding the grassy edge difficult.

"Use the water gate steps," Bertie called. "Just come this way. The steps will find you."

Tori slipped off her crate and treaded water behind Kale. "Go in front—I can't walk up in my underwear in front of those two."

"No problem. Just stay behind me, then make a run for the bushes."

He swam to the steps wondering why he hadn't noticed them the previous day. He found his answer on step three. The steps were covered with long hairy moss, and were very slippery. One step and he skidded back into the Evenlode.

From there he saw Bertie's eyes widen as Tori rose up like Bottlicelli's Venus—a pale goddess of the sea come to life.

Harry was quick with a robe, and had two words for Bertie, "Stop ogling!"

Harry's concern for Tori's modesty stood as a good sign; it was almost fatherly. Her image hung in Kale's mind like a lantern as she hurried into the shadows to dry off.

Harry shone his oversized flashlight on the cable strung across the Evenlode. Five crates already bobbed there like corralled heifers. Kale splashed water at Harry and began shepherding them ashore. "How many did you toss in?"

"Are you serious? I threw in all the crates. I'm betting every bottle's worth a thousand pounds!"

Kale gasped, coughed, and set to work pushing them to where Harry could haul them up to Bertie who stacked them into a neat pile. He saw Tori join, wearing the robe tied tight around her waist. "Hey, Harry, this is just exercise for you," she yelled, and settled down beside Bertie.

Kale attacked the work with the fervor of a man needing emancipating from his fantasies.

Monday morning, and a roost of noisy rooks woke Kale from dreamland. "Stupid birds," he muttered and tried to reacclimatize himself. This was not the Priory. This was an upper bedroom of Bertillon Manor: big room, big bed, a huge wall of moldy books. Even in all the bigness he felt claustrophobic. "Need fresh air. Oh, my head. It smells like a jam factory in here." The cloying aroma of raspberry hung in the air like mist. He rolled from the huge bed, staggered toward the wall of high leaded windows and with some difficulty threw one open.

"Never, never another raspberry," he swore aloud, and breathed deeply of the rain-freshened air until his head stopped spinning. His new room provided a good view of the Evenlode and even with a blanket of ground fog he could see the two hundred and twelve crates of Mary's best that Tori and Bertie had piled into a rather shoddy looking pyramid. Kale suffered a painful flashback of trying to climb to the top. Then he laughed remembering that except for two crates reserved for Tori, the whole pile now belonged to Bertie. Last night, after they'd finished carting and stacking, Harry, in a fit of genius had traded their share of the found booty for Bertillon Manor. The place had three new owners and it hadn't cost them a cent. "Just think of it, Bertie," Harry had wheedled, "you'll have every bottle of the old liqueur to sell at the Priory. What a drawing card. And after Kale and Tori get their book written, your place will be famous. We all have a claim to this booty, but if it has to go to court the government will grab the lot and leave us all in the cold. Bloody best deal of the century, Bertie. And all it will cost you is that pile of stone you want rid of anyway."

Bertie hadn't the breath to answer fast enough. "Right! It's a deal, but I won't be keeping them for the Priory. I'm selling all but a small private stock. With the cash, I'll bloody well refurbish the inn. Open a few of those bottles, Kale! We'll drink to the success of Wychwood Spirits and the new home of Galley Press! It's a good life that has your friends living close by. Let us drink to being friends always."

Tori screamed and ran about with tears running down like rivers. Her impossible dream had come true. Despite the excitement, Kale had retained reservations; the place was in very poor condition. But now, in the light of early morning, he had to admit Harry had done well. Galley Press did indeed have a new home and everybody seemed happy. He stuck his head out the window and yelled, "You're a genius, Harry Bass."

Like a reminder of the deal's shortcomings, a stream of water suddenly poured down his neck from the leaks in the ceiling. Quilt-wrapped and groaning, he stumbled to the bathroom only to find that his shower dribbled ice water. Maybe it wasn't such a good deal. They were still broke, and now they had this monster fixer-upper to deal with.

Shivering and feeling ill, he walked out the door of his new room and counted one hundred and twelve paces to the kitchen, to where Harry and Tori sat nibbling fried bread and discussing fence and barn construction. Kale declined her offer to fry more bloaters. He would never eat anything called a bloater even if it was only sausage. He settled for buttered toast and a glass of unidentifiable citrus juice that tasted of can and reminded him of the metal box in the stream. "There was an iron box, Harry. Right where you pushed me in. I think we should go have a look."

"Fine place to hide a diamond," Harry said.

Tori sighed. "Okay. We'll give it another go. But if anything should happen to me, be warned I shall haunt the both of you."

The decision of when to return to the cellar was left for later when a car horn sounded from the car park. Bertie and his wine appraiser had arrived, and behind them came a large van.

Outside, with his forehead pasted on the roof of Harry's car for coolness, Kale listened to the appraiser assure Bertie that his antique liqueur could indeed be auctioned off for very large sums. Bertie handled everything very well and even managed to fend off the appraiser's questions as to why the cases were stacked outside, and in such a manner. "We thought to make it easier for the box men." Kale thought that a very good answer. Then the box men loaded the cases into the lorry and were soon packed up and gone. Kale overheard the departing wine appraiser mention a figure of two thousand pounds per bottle. Yes, Uncle Bertie had done well for himself, and had still kept aside a good portion for the Priory. The truck's dust hadn't cleared when down the lane came the Bertillon family solicitor with the deed and a stack of papers he'd kept ready on his computer at Bertie's request for the speedy sale of the place at first notice.

By noon, the manor had officially changed ownership and the happy group escorted the solicitor outside. About to get into his car, the man turned and inquired about the new name of the manor. Kale was quick with his response, "Victoria. Victoria Manor."

Harry smiled and nodded, Bertie smiled and nodded, and Tori's eyes once again streamed tears like rivers.

"Victoria Manor it is. I shall have that duly registered. Must be off now, good-bye, and good luck all. Lady Roche, I shall forward all the pertinent documents for your records."

Tori spun around, eyes searching for a stranger.

The solicitor chuckled. "A little bonus for you, Victoria. If I may be so bold to call you that?"

"What?"

Kale shook his head; Tori could sometimes be so abrupt.

"The title goes with the estate."

"You mean, Bertie will simply be plain Bertie? No, no. I don't want that."

"Can't be helped. Well, toodle-loo! You'll be hearing from me." He climbed into his chauffeured Rolls Royce and went off waving out the window.

Bertie laughed. "Heavens, Victoria, don't worry about me, I'd much rather be rich than royal. Anyway, I won't have time for silly things. When I returned to the hotel last night, I found there had been a riot by the guests. The reception area and dining room are ruined. I guess it's just as well, since I'm going to remodel.

"I've been thinking of a better plan," Harry said. Walking to his car he returned holding Mary Gant's leather-bound formula book with all Mary's recipes except for the potent one due back to the monks. "Here's your better idea, Bertie: the Wychwood Spirit formulas. Open a small distillery at the rear of the hotel."

"Bloody terrific!" Bertie flipped through the book, his face lighting more and more with every page turned. "I owe you, friends. I shall find you the best roofer in the land."

Tori laughed. "I only hope he proves better than the fellow who's been doing your patches."

Excited, and wanting to make a plan for the distillery, Bertie set off in his car for the Priory. Harry paced off an area for a horse barn, and Kale joined Tori on a jog around their new property.

The ground was soft from a recent rain, but the result was lush grass and the heavy, refreshing fragrance of foliage. Heather grew in the fields. The old wooden fences, though useless, added a sense of history to the rolling expanse. The river surface danced with sunlight, and a mist curled along its edge imbuing the whole scene with a magical quality.

Skirting the Roll Round Stones, they chose a worn path through the great oaks that edged the meadow behind the manor. The quiet beauty inspired Kale to catch hold of Tori's hand and pull her to a stop.

With a slight bow, he kissed that hand. "Lady Victoria, this manor was named most aptly, a land swathed in beauty, as are you. I—"

She pulled her hand away. "You know, I simply can't wait to show this place to my family." Then she laughed, which put him completely off his proposal.

"Race you to the manor," she yelled and bolted off across the meadow, dispersing mist like a sprite.

He sighed, and followed at a jog.

Returning to the manor, they found Harry waiting with bad tidings. Chief Inspector Slagin had dropped by with news that the dead body of Bertie's amiable bartender had been hauled off the weir at the village of Oddington. "That's six or seven miles down river from here," Harry said. "Slagin hadn't seen the body yet, but was told on the phone by the local doctor that there appeared to be nothing to indicate foul play."

Tori and Kale, still out of breath, lost their giddy grins as if slapped by reality.

"I rather liked that bartender," Tori mumbled.

Tori's face paled and Kale realized the deaths were taking more of a toll on her than she would admit. He felt the same way. He took her hand.

Harry walked around in agitated circles. "We ought to return to the Priory before someone discovers the stairs under the brazier. I closed the brazier over the opening, but we had better check it out. It's not as hard to move now that the rust and crud have been shaken loose."

Kale scowled at him, but realized death was routine for Harry. Maybe it was best if they pressed on without dwelling on it. "All right, then, let's go."

In the car heading toward the Priory, the trio discussed the barman and arrived at three scenarios for his sudden demise: One, the bartender had spotted the hole under the brazier, had gone down into the cellar and fallen through the slate, just like Tori. Two, somebody had shoved him into the Evenlode. Three, the bartender had gone to Mary's club and stumbled across Abner Snow's men digging a hole in the cellar floor.

Harry liked the second theory.

"I like the last one," Kale said.

Except for the two cars in the hotel car park, Wychwood looked like a ghost town. The three bolted for the front door and through to the hotel kitchen. The brazier looked untouched and Kale was overjoyed, for he wanted no responsibility in the barman's death. All three put shoulders to the heavy slate bowl and pushed. It opened easily now, but with a loud grating noise.

Harry whispered, "Quiet, I hear something."

Kale heard it too. Voices.

Chapter Twelve

"**Y**ou two stay here. I'll go down and have a look."
Kale grabbed a flashlight, slid past the brazier, and
crept down the narrow steps into the hidden cellar of
the Priory. The voices emanated from the hole like a
loudspeaker and were coming closer. Harry had been
wrong to assume no one would be foolhardy enough to
enter that fast-moving stream. Keeping low, he scurried
across to where Tori had fallen through the slate. Dropping onto his belly, he stuck his head into the hole and
saw a rope directly below. The smell of the river, fresh
and heavy with earth, enveloped his senses. Flashing
lights glared in his face. He pulled up a bit, out of range
of the lights, and listened. A deep voice boomed out,
"Hey Mr. Snow, we're almost at the end. I can see a
hole."

Kale scrambled to his feet and retreated back to the
steps. Racing to the top, he said, "We have real prob-

lems! Abner and his goons must have found the stream before it went underground. They dropped in a float tied to a very long rope. Right now he and his gang are pulling themselves across from the church. They're almost here!"

They hurried down, and true to her ever-curious nature Tori stuck her head down the hole beside Harry's. "Ingenious! I should have thought of it."

Harry smiled and muttered something about Abner being too smart for his own good. He pulled a trusty clasp knife from his pocket, flopped onto his belly and reached into the hole to swiftly cut through Abner's line.

Abner screamed. Kale and Tori laughed. "But we have to give him credit, Kale. To think of finding the stream on the surface was smart."

"Right. And there's another smart guy. I wonder what this one's up to?" He pointed to the squat shadow scurrying along beside the slate stream cover toward the far end of the cellar.

Harry reeled in twenty feet of Abner Snow's rope and sliced it neatly in half with his knife. He motioned to Kale, who picked up the free end of the rope.

"Tie it around your waist," he said.

"Me? Why me? I've been in that stream already. You haven't even touched the water!"

Tori arrived at his side. "Don't be silly Kale, Harry is too old to be playing around in cold water. If you won't go, give it to me." Her eyes twinkled a challenge.

Kale had half a mind to let her go. He even pretended to hand her the rope, but snatched it back. There was no way he would let her, and she knew it.

Easing himself through the hole, his feet barely touching the rocky ledge, he slipped into the icy water. Once again it took his breath away, and even with Harry pulling hard on the rope he found the current forcing him to grapple with the stony ledge. A last scream from one of Abner's men echoed through the tunnel. One of them must have hung up on the fruit press drive shaft under the church.

Kale dove under and located the metal box, but Harry hauled him to the surface four times before he finally managed to slip the rope through the handle at one end. His hands felt frozen and detached as he clumsily worked the rope into a knot. At last, the box was ready to haul up.

Harry's voice rang out from the hole up above. "Get up here and help me pull!"

Gasping for air as he climbed from the water, he heard Harry yell again. "Hurry now, Kale. Grab hold and pull for all you're worth. Hurry!" An unnecessary instruction, for Kale knew Abner would check the rope and was probably already pulling for shore with murder on his mind. Thoughts of an angry Hermes Wheems gave him the strength of Hercules.

Minutes passed too quickly. They used five just to land their catch, and that much again to muscle the dripping box—as hefty in size as a decent beach cooler, but far heavier and rough with rust—up the cellar steps and down the hallway to the front door. Behind them, a trail of water marked their path. Almost running, they heaved the box into the open boot of Harry's car and slammed it shut. Like an answer to a prayer, rain began to spatter around them, washing their wet trail into oblivion. Harry had the motor revved and the car moving before Tori and Kale had even shut their doors.

The big Mercedes sped off in a cloud of rubber smoke with Kale looking out the back window. Almost out of sight, he spotted a half-dozen tiny shadows meandering across the road. "We beat them, Harry! But that was too close for comfort. One of these days you'll get us killed and be very sorry for it."

Harry barked out a strange hissing laugh.

"Harry?" Kale listened, astounded.

"Cartoon laugh," Tori said turning in her seat. "Haven't you ever heard his cartoon laugh? Show us the laughing dog, Harrykins."

Harry laughed even louder, and it did sound like the cartoon hound that always ran to the end of his rope. "Foghorn Leghorn's dog," Kale murmured, and, looking at Harry he began to laugh too, so hard he couldn't get air and had to roll the window down. Stress did strange things to people. Rain drizzled down his already wet face.

The laugh got the better of Harry. As he turned into the manor's narrow drive he missed and caught a yew hedge with the rear bumper.

Kale opened the window and looked back. "Harry, slow down! You're dragging a big hunk of hedge behind the car."

"The drive needed widening anyway. It's always

scratching my car." He said it so seriously, Tori exploded into a fit of laughter.

Inside the manor, Harry made opening the rusty strongbox a bit like Christmas and insisted they wait for Kale to change into dry clothes. Then he suggested to Tori that food and drink on the coffee table might be a good idea, and busied himself building a fire in the monstrous old fireplace.

"Only a small fire, Harry," Tori insisted. "I heard noises when I swept the hearth. Maybe rats."

Harry glanced up to see if she was serious, smiled, then muttered something about getting them out and began feeding logs to the fire like it was a locomotive.

By the time Kale had shucked his wets and returned wearing a dry sweater and jeans, heat had risen in the great hall and flames were licking at the damp air of the living room. "What's with the inferno? Harry planning to melt some gold?"

Tori shrugged and handed him a cup of tea.

"Anything to eat?"

Tori held out a can of mixed cocktail nuts. "This is the last in the cupboard. We'll have to shop tomorrow."

Harry shuffled back from the fire, grabbed hold of the strongbox, and pulled it closer to the roaring flames. The dull rusted box came alive in the glow of the fire and Kale and Harry both noticed the remains of an intricate design beneath the crud, a series of red and black insignia running the length and width of each side. For a moment, Kale stood perplexed thinking Harry was intent on drying the box to reveal more of it, until his attention was drawn to the ceiling and the sound of running feet.

"Rats!" Tori yelled. "I told you I heard them."

Kale knew better. He turned and ran cross the great hall, took the stairs three at a time, and galloped down the hall toward the Norman tower. He could hear heavy feet pounding across the catwalk and arrived there gasping for air. Baffled by the trespassers' quick disappearing act, Kale crossed to the east wing and walked the hall back and forth listening for the slightest sound. Almost back at the catwalk he spotted a sooty footprint on the threadbare carpet. The large print pointed directly at a bedroom door. He turned the knob and gave the door a shove. The room looked empty, but when he leaned in for a quick check something cracked across his skull, folding him onto the floor like an accordion.

Sprawled there, unable to move, he heard Tori calling, "Where are you, Kale? Kale?"

Slowly, painfully, he sat upright. Too stunned to reply, he could only wish she would hurry; he felt lightheaded and drifting, hanging on by a thread. Then he heard a horrible cry from outside. "Some kind of animal," he whispered, and everything went black.

"Kale! Wake up!" Tori yelled, slapping him.

He came around sharply. "Hey, cut that out! You're not supposed to slap unconscious people. What if I have a concussion?" He reached for the tender spot on the top of his head. "Ouch! Feels like he used an anvil. Did you see him?"

"Who? I didn't see anybody. Here, let me rub it for you."

"Ow! I can't believe I fell for the old behind-the-

door trick. I stuck my head in and got bopped!" Kale
indicated the footprint pointing toward the bedroom
door and rubbed his head.

"A Wellie made that," she said. "A very big boot."

"Do you know if Hermes Wheems wears Welling-
tons?"

"No. I've never seen him out of his truck."

"Yes you did! You saw him on the roof of Mary's
church."

"He was too far away. Now let's get you onto your
feet. Whoever it was is probably still here. We had better get Harry."

Tori helped Kale back down the stairs, stumbling under the weight of him despite her height. Kale smiled at
the thought. It felt good to have her arms wrapped around
him. He should have thought of playing wounded earlier.

Harry stood by the front window, curtain held aside,
staring at the squeaky wheeled lorry heading down the
driveway at breakneck speed. "Exit Hermes Wheems,
our rat."

"My assailant," corrected Kale as Tori helped him
ease into an armchair.

"Good grief! What happened to you?" Harry strode
across looking grave.

"He crowned me, a good one too."

Tori looked from Kale to Harry and down to the
metal box, she raised an eyebrow. "Harry, tell me you
haven't gone and opened it?"

Harry shrugged and nodded toward the box. "The
lock is off. I've been waiting for you." He bent over it
and with an anticipatory pause, opened the strongbox.

Kale leaned over in his chair and peered into the box. His jaw fell. The contents were reminiscent of the stacks of antique mother-of-pearl poker chips his Yale fraternity had numbered among its proudest possessions, but they didn't have nearly as many.

"What are these things?" Tori asked. She dropped to her knees and began searching through the mound of pearly discs. "Look at them all. There must be thousands, but no diamond. Harry what are these?" She picked one from the pile and held it to the fire where it shone rainbow colors like an opal. "Harry?"

"Those are gambling chips, Tori, not the treasure."

"Poker chips? Well, that means—"

In a fit of pique, Harry threw his glass into the fireplace. "It means someone else already knew about the stream, the liquor, and whatever kind of gambling house Mary had going. If the diamond was hidden down there, they've already searched for it. Your diamond is probably just a bloody memory." Harry reached into the box for a handful of the pearly discs and scattered them into the roaring fire. "Bloody pile of worthless clam shells," he shouted.

"Harry!" Tori yelled and covered the box with her body.

"I wouldn't say exactly worthless," Kale said reaching down for a handful. "My school fraternity hosts a poker tournament every year. It's been tradition for over a century and a half. We use chips just like these, although I think these are in better condition. Our last insurance appraisal had them valued at seventy-five dollars."

"Each?" Harry said, astounded.

"Yes, each!"

Harry wasn't wasting any time. Down went the lid of the strongbox and back went the two hasps.

"I'll take it into the city right now. I have a friend at Sotheby's that I can knock up. He'll give me an appraisal and the name of a buyer. If you're even just half-right, Kale, it'll mean we can start putting a roof on this leaky mausoleum."

"Tell the truth Harry." interjected Tori, smiling. "What you really mean is you can start building your horse barn and fences with a clear conscience."

"Tori Roche, you're too smart by half. Now you two take one end, we'll get this into the Mercedes and I'll be off to see a man about a horse."

Tori laughed all the way to the front door and only stopped when she saw the rain teeming down. "I'll stay here and keep watch, thank you very much."

Kale helped load the chest into the boot of Harry's car and then stood in the pouring rain listening to his last minute instructions. Moments later he ran and joined Tori under the shelter of the doorway where she stood waving at the departing Mercedes.

"I wonder if he'll really stop and see a man about a horse," Kale said walking into the warmth of the great hall. "What did Harry call our new palace—a mausoleum? What nerve."

"But a sweet one, Kale. And I told you before, he sometimes does see a man about a horse, but mostly I think he just reports into work. And don't ask me who he works for. Our Harry is very closemouthed about his retirement. What did he say to you?"

"Nothing much. He told me if Hermes Wheems returned, I was to shoot first and ask questions later. He gave me this." Kale reached a hand around to his back pocket and brought out a small handgun.

"A pistol! You don't think Wheems will come back, do you?"

"I certainly do."

Tori moved back across the entrance hall through to the great fireplace. "Why do you suppose those poker chips were in the river?"

"I think whoever killed Mary Gant threw her into the river and the poker chips in after her. But let's look on the bright side; she's left us thousands of those poker chips, and they might be worth enough to get us a start on the roof," Kale.

Tori smiled wanly, her usual enthusiasm lacking. "I think it's all rather disappointing. Mary's diamond would have been like a helping hand for this place. I fear Harry's right; it is nothing but an old drafty mausoleum. Mary's diamond would have made it a home."

He watched despair seep into her eyes.

She continued. "We could have repaired the roof, put a new floor in the tower, put down new carpets, new wiring and plumbing. Oh Kale, what have I done? I convinced you and Harry to buy this place and now we're in a deeper hole. Galley Press is more in debt and headquartered in a big, leaky white elephant. I'm as foolish as my father. We never should have traded with Bertie. Think of the taxes on this place."

Kale pulled his ear until it hurt. Taxes? He hadn't even considered taxes.

"The overhead will kill us."

"You're forgetting the insurance money and the offer Neddy got for the property. That should help."

Tori plopped down on the old sofa, sinking deep into the worn-out cushions. "Phooey! Inland Revenue will scoop it all. Have you forgotten we still owe them for Tulley's tax transgressions? Why do you think the insurance company agreed to pay up so quickly? They know the government wants the money. We'll be doing business in a leaky old mausoleum with Inland Revenue hanging about like vultures waiting for every post. If we had the funds to option a good manuscript we could have a fighting chance. I had prospects picked from our slush pile, but now even that went up in flames."

"Well, we have to hope Harry does all right with the chips."

"Phooey on that too! Who in their right mind would pay good money for old clamshells? No, we're doomed, I just know it."

"We could sell the boxes of liqueur. We have two crates of that in the kitchen."

"No! That liqueur is my gift to you and Harry for helping me. Besides, it wouldn't bring in enough to pay for one sheet of roofing copper. Besides, the Sotheby's auction will put it on the market as a drug. No, we won't sell. We'll save it for special occasions, to remember Mary Gant and what it cost her."

Kale stretched out at her feet and they chased away despondency by sharing a fireside dinner of mixed nuts and hot tea.

Kale watched Tori's face in the flickering firelight. The setting gave her an exotic air. He re-conjured the vision of her rising goddess-like from the river, and tightened with the desperate need to hold her.

Despite how well he knew her, she remained as mysterious and deep as the day they met. Tonight's disappointment was one of the few inner glimpses she gave of how dearly she wanted to prove herself in the world. Tori tended to wear a mask of success, hoping life would meet her halfway. For the most part, she succeeded. But he wanted to be that one special someone she could open her heart to, the person with whom she could share both success and failure. He didn't want her to act happy in front of him; he wanted her to *be* happy with him.

Egged on by her quiet mood and the romance of the fire, he stepped toward the sofa. He thought he would just settle in beside her and stretch his arm around her shoulders, just the most casual of intimacies; a step forward to show her how serious he was. He would tell her honestly of his intentions and promise her exactly what she wanted about rebuilding this old pile of bricks and fill her head with visions of them being famous novelists of the most well-acclaimed work. Maybe she would fall into his arms with eager kisses.

Another step and he was at the couch, bending down, taking his place beside her. She didn't move or mock him or slide over as he lowered himself at her side.

His weight sank the cushion farther into the springy bottom and toppled Tori into his lap. Tea splashed across her as she rolled onto the floor, laughing.

"Sorry, old excuse of a sofa."

Tori giggled and shifted into unstoppable laughter. She stood and began twirling to an unheard rhythm and seconds later flopped into his lap.

He looked into her eyes and saw a trusting soul, a partner. He kissed her gently, "Let's get you changed."

She sighed at his words, as if playing a theatre part. "Can I wear one of your Yale sweaters?"

He pushed himself off the sofa, got her onto her feet and pulled her through the door to the great staircase. At the top, Tori's change of clothes was suddenly forgotten.

"Kale, if it really was Wheems that conked you on the bean, how did he get outside? He certainly didn't get out by the stairs. I would have seen him."

Kale squinted at her. What had happened to the mood between them?

She pulled her hand away, her eyes glittering with excitement. "Maybe he used a secret passage?"

"What?"

"The scoundrel that conked you on the head."

"Wheems?"

"Or somebody driving his truck. Whoever it was, he had to get out somehow. Kale, we must have a look for it. I do love secret doors and passages. Bertie is so lucky."

They pounded walls up and down the long hallway for an hour, crossed to the east wing and searched for another hour. Then they searched every nook and cranny of the room where Kale's assailant had been hiding. They found nothing.

"I'm pooped," Tori said. "I'm going down to change. I'll be back."

"Come back up to my room when you're done."

He trudged down the hall to his own room and rooted through a jumble of papers looking for the Mary Gant journal. He wanted to check for any overlooked hints about the diamond. It wasn't there. Thinking he'd stuck it among the many molding books on the shelves, he turned and glimpsed at the spines. His glance wandered upward to the topmost shelves as he read titles. A faded red one caught his eye. He hadn't noticed it before: *A History of Wychwood,* it read. Interesting.

As he reached for it, Tori arrived, comfortable in fuzzy slippers and a soft, clingy sweater over blue jeans. "Oh!" she exclaimed, "I expected your room to be like mine. But it's not at all. You have a much larger fireplace and a whole wall of moldy books. Kale, they smell bad."

"Wonderful, isn't it?" he said. "And I only have to walk a hundred extra steps to get here."

She frowned at his exaggeration and ran her finger down a book spine and read the title aloud, "*Roxana.* Good story. Oh, and here's *Moll Flanders.* Too bad they're such a mess. I adore Defoe's inspirational books, especially *Robinson Crusoe.* She pulled the last title from the shelf, flipped the book open, and began to read.

" 'One day, about noon, going toward my boat, I was exceedingly surprised with the print of a man's naked foot on the shore, which was very plain to be seen on the sand.' That's hope in a nutshell, and no author has ever put it onto a page quite as well."

He watched, amused.

"I should have this room," she said.

He grinned. "I'll share it anytime you like."

She tossed him a not-very-likely smile.

The history book forgotten, Kale walked to his bedside table and picked up a copy of Longfellow's "Hiawatha." "Look at this." He pointed to the copyright: 1895. "Not a first edition, but old enough to be worth a good buck."

One sniff and Tori handed it back. "Bertie should be horsewhipped for allowing these books to rot."

Moving along the shelf, Kale was startled to see a copy of Lewis Carroll's *Through the Looking Glass.* That such a fantasy should repose among so many staid authors was intriguing. The story of my life in England, he thought. He pulled it toward him, thinking to lay it aside for a night's read. Only it wouldn't budge. When he leaned in to examine why, he discovered it wasn't a book at all, only a spine, and was attached to a kind of pulley. He pulled it again, harder this time, and was somehow not surprised that it opened a section of shelving.

"You've found it!" Tori squealed. "A secret door!"

Chapter Thirteen

Peering into the secret passageway, Kale remembered the animal cry he heard earlier and the words of Lord Caddington's rhymed warning, *I think we better go down and have a look. But be very careful.* He moved the narrow door back and forth on silent hinges. "Somebody has oiled these, and not too long ago. I don't think it will lock behind us. You stay well behind. And watch your step."

Dark, narrow, and very steep, the stairs wound down to the dead end of a stone wall.

"Kale, that's my loo on the other side. My toilet runs, I can hear it. And look! Those are the pipes. No, it couldn't be . . ."

It was. The tiny concealed door opened with just a push, and Kale found himself looking into a small bathroom similar to his. The door was small. Getting through required some near-acrobatic contortions.

"This rather puts me off Wheems being your head bopper, Kale. He would have to have one of Alice's make-me-small potions to pop through this rabbit hole. Here, give me a hand."

Inside her room, she demanded Kale fix a lock onto the rabbit hole, and with a sweep of her arm toward the stack of boxes that had been delivered that day, she insisted on a swap of rooms. "Look at all these cartons. They're all my books. I need a room with shelves. You don't have any books. Well, not any books without mold."

Kale didn't listen; he was too busy examining the two walls of leaded windows, looking for the one used by his assailant. He found it at the very end, an open window with a sole print clearly defined on the sill. He leaned out. "Tori! There's somebody lying in the grass down there."

"What?"

Running for the door and fumbling Harry's pistol from his back pocket, he yelled, "C'mon! Let's get down there. But stay behind me."

The man lying facedown in the wet grass was not dead. Not yet. Pocketing the pistol, Kale crouched down to help Tori roll him over.

"It's the gardener from the Priory," she whispered.

"He does look like a gnome."

Unkempt and stinking of raspberry, the old man groaned and opened one beady eye. Kale saw him actually try to smile as Tori set about examining his head wound.

"Kale, the whole side of his head is caved in, and

he's lost a lot of blood. Quick, give me your pullover. I'll try and stop the bleeding. You run and call for an ambulance, quickly!"

On his feet, through the neckhole of his favorite sweatshirt, Kale saw the old man raise an arm and point a bloody finger at the manor. "Horse buns!" he shouted and started up a bubbly sounding laugh that ended abruptly in a great whoosh of raspberry redolent breath.

"Never mind the shirt. He's dead," Tori whispered. "He must have jumped from my window and hit his head on that boulder."

Kale looked at the rock and saw blood. He leaned down, looked into the gardener's lifeless eyes and closed them. "I'll go and call the police." He turned and started for the front door.

"Call Chief Inspector Jeremy Slagin," Tori yelled. "I wrote his number in the book by the telephone."

Victoria Manor looked like a madhouse of activity. Blue lights winked, car doors slammed, cameras flashed, and it continued until daylight edged over the horizon.

"Where is Harry Bass?" Kale had fielded that same question a dozen times already. His head ached and his stomach kept up a constant growl for lack of food. As the sun peeked over the great oaks, he demanded Slagin let Tori go to the market. "We're hungry, thirsty, and we've nothing to eat in this house. We could all use some coffee."

Slagin suggested Tori try the store at Oddington. "It

opens early to provision tourists fishing the Evenlode River below the village. They have a good selection of fine foods. It's where that barkeep was employed before he hired on with Lord Bertillon." Slagin even volunteered a man to drive her.

Kale returned Tori's departing wave from the police car and turned to watch Bertie, who'd only just been dragged from his bed at the Priory.

"Really," Bertie complained, "pulled from my bed to identify some poor blighter who would still be dead at a decent hour."

Kale stayed off to the side as Bertie approached the corpse.

Bertie leaned over and shook his head. "Yes, that is my gardener James Potter. Drunk most of the time, but he could keep a garden better than most. Why does he smell like raspberry jam?"

Slagin was zeroing in on Bertie like a prowling cat when a white truck came squeaking down the lane.

"My roof man," Bertie said, and ran off to avoid further questioning.

Kale stared at the truck in total disbelief. Hermes Wheems slowly dismounted from the cab with a box of tools gripped in his left hand. Dirty overalls made him look every inch a roof man, but he had the darting, troubled eyes of a mental patient.

Kale sauntered up behind Bertie with Slagin stuck to his side like bubble gum. Keeping to the game, he allowed himself to be introduced to Wheems, and even shook the giant's hand, hiding his disgust.

Wheems grunted, hauled down a thick, compact ladder and headed off toward the front door looking as if he knew the way. Bertie followed, but only after a few whispered words to Kale, "He looks scary, but he really is the best roof man, and Harry told me to hire the best."

Kale groaned and followed Slagin to the front door, only to stop when an ambulance arrived to haul off the late Mr. Potter. Kale was sure Wheems had something to do with the foul deed and was considering what to do next when Slagin put an arm on his shoulder. The chief inspector's expression turned grim.

"We have a little problem, Mr. Kale. Perhaps you can help us. That rock, the one that dented in the gardener's skull, well, that came from somewhere else. We can't find another one like it on this property, and we've searched everywhere. Mr. Kale, I have a feeling you know where that rock came from. Do you?"

Kale shrugged. "I haven't the slightest idea."

Slagin nodded patiently and again demanded answers for the raspberry smell, Harry's whereabouts, and what the gardener had meant by shouting, "Horse buns."

Kale shrugged in response to all three.

"You and Tori might have been better off staying home last night."

"We are home. We bought this place."

Slagin slapped him on the shoulder. "That's fantastic! I live just below Oddington. That makes us almost neighbors." Looking up, he shook his head and added, "You'll be needing to fix the roof. All these old manor houses need roof repair."

Kale wondered how much jail-time a sock in the eye would fetch.

"Right! I'll be off then. Mind you don't leave the area without giving us a ring. Good day, Mr. Kale. Ah, looks like you have more company coming."

An old beat-up Volkswagen of indeterminate color slid to a dusty stop. Never having set eyes on his receptionist's mode of transportation, Kale was surprised to see Neddy exit from the old beetle.

"Neddy! You are a sight for sore eyes."

He hauled two suitcases from the back seat while she ran around to the front and took three more from the boot. "Okay. I'm ready to see my room."

She looked different. Her hair hung in thin wrinkled waves to her waist and she wore a bright blue sweatshirt with jeans so tight he wondered how she managed to sit. She looked so totally different from her office persona that he felt dizzy recompiling her image. Harry was right, he did tend to picture people in stereotype.

"What's wrong?" Neddy asked. "Tori told me to be here at eight. And here I am, right on time. Didn't you know I was coming? Isn't my room ready? Of course this isn't all my stuff. I have two more trunks at the old place. That's all I could fit this trip. I'll make another dash back next week."

"Tori must have forgotten to tell me."

"Oh well, that's Tori for you. Now that you know, let's get a move on. I've got work to do."

Dazed, he carried four of Neddy's five bags to the second floor and told her to pick a bedroom not already occupied. "We have lots."

"Which one is Harry's?"

"North wing, at the front. Right down there."

"Good. I'll take north wing, at the back. You can leave those bags, I'll take them from here." Her eyes, freed from the black frames of her reading glasses, sparkled with excitement. Kale watched her grab up two bags and wobble off down the hall in very unpractical shoes.

He pulled his ear again, wondering how he'd never caught on to her interest in Harry before. Was it reciprocated? He thought again of the roses Harry always brought to the office. Kale had always assumed he'd bought the extra bouquet for Neddy only to be diplomatic. Could those casual lunchtime exits of Harry and Neddy's have been a budding romance? He'd never looked at Neddy as anything other than an efficient secretary, but now. . . . "I'm an idiot," he said to himself.

Shaking his head, he turned and started down the stairs. He was deep in thought about Harry and Neddy when the doorbell rang. He hurried down the remaining stairs and threw open the door. Harry's barn and fence men stood there looking impatient for Harry. For the umpteenth time Kale denied knowing his whereabouts.

"We need to unload," said one.

"Down by the river," and Kale leaned out and pointed.

Later that evening as they sat down for dinner, Harry arrived wearing a new blue Armani suit, and bearing gifts, which he presented with a great flourish. "Chocolates for the ladies, cigars for you, Kale." Two boxes of chocolates—Harry had expected Neddy's presence.

Neddy accepted the gift with her usual business-like nod, and Tori gave him a peck on the cheek.

"Genuine Cuban cigars, Kale," Harry said, and in a whisper adding that Castro used to be partial to Cohibas.

"Harry, I don't smoke."

"These don't count as smoking. Cohibas are an experience."

Neddy wagged a finger. "You boys experience those things outside after dinner. Harry, go wash your hands."

Harry went off grumbling like a small boy.

Wow. They were like an old married couple and he'd never noticed it before. Suddenly more comfortable with Tori, he reached over and rifled her chocolates for hard centers.

Harry stomped back, held up his hands for Neddy's approval, and beamed ear to ear when she placed a giant shepherd's pie on the table. Even hearing about finding the corpse of the gardener couldn't keep Harry from his pie.

"Murdered?" He stopped squirting ketchup. "Are you sure?"

Tori nodded, "Scotland Yard is quite sure, Harry."

Harry replied with the name of the obvious candidate. "Abner Snow."

Tori rolled her eyes in disbelief.

Kale cleared his throat, "Actually, I think Slagin has me pegged as the prime suspect."

Harry dug into his inside pocket and produced a stack of bills thick enough to choke a horse. "Mother of pearl chips bring lots of the ready green these days."

Between spoonfuls of shepherd's pie, he dove back into his pocket for an even bigger stack of . . . ready green.

Neddy shoved her plate aside. "Come to mother, you dirty little darlings; you're going to put the Press back into business.

Kale said, "I don't think Abner Snow had anything to do with the gardener's death."

Harry shrugged, spooned up pie, and used his next ketchup pause to inquire after his fence and barn men.

Tori laughed. "Yes, Harrykins, your barn men were here and unloaded a whopping batch of heavy machinery down by the river. Work begins tomorrow."

After dinner Harry and Kale lit up and puffed their way around to the scene of the grisly crime using the two large flashlights Tori had brought from the shop at Oddington. The moonless night carried a chill and the grass felt damp underfoot.

Harry gave a loud belch and bent his stubby frame to examine the murder scene. "What did Potter mean when he shouted, 'Horse buns,' and why did he point at the manor? Where did he get the raspberry liqueur? What was he doing here?"

Kale gave the same shrug he gave the chief inspector. When the subject turned to the pistol Harry had given him, Kale explained that he hadn't mentioned it to Slagin, and that yes, he did know how to shoot the thing.

Harry thought about that a few seconds and walked over to examine the wall of the manor.

Kale watched his friend go over every stone. Harry

looked over his shoulder. "Strange looking hole here. I think it takes a key. You still have it with you, the gun?"

Grinning, Kale pulled it from his back pocket only to endure Harry's rolling eyes. "Shoot into the hole, but wait until I get far enough out of the way. Shoot at an angle."

Raised on a visual diet of American TV and witness to hundreds of locks shot off doors, Kale thought nothing of this task. He stepped close, took aim, and fired. He fired again, only this time, the wall bounced the bullet back. Falling, gasping for a breath that wouldn't come, Kale had one parting thought—*horse buns*.

Chapter Fourteen

"**Y**ou're not shot."

Harry's words interrupted Kale's dream of hometown girls and butterscotch ripple ice cream.

"Wake up! The bullet just bounced back and hit your lamp. Breathe deeply, and stop being a baby. Get on your feet, we have work to do."

Feeling like he had been kicked by a horse, Kale allowed Harry to help him to his feet. "Why didn't you warn me?"

"I did! I told you to shoot on an angle. Here, keep it for a souvenir. Now, let's go!"

Kale examined the flattened pellet and stuck it into his pocket. Then he took a deep breath and wobbled after his stubby friend through a gap in the wall of Victoria Manor, an opening he had watched appear like magic while firing the second shot. He paused to examine the ancient locking mechanism, now smashed and dangling from a single screw. "Harry! Wait up! I don't have my flashlight."

Without even a slice of helpful moonlight, Kale stepped down into the abyss of the black yawning hole. "Harry!" Kale's voice echoed. "How did you know that keyhole was there?"

"You told me."

"No I didn't."

"You told me the gardener pointed at the wall before he died."

"That's right, I did. It never entered my mind he was pointing at something."

"I'll say it again, that's why I'm the detective and you're the writer."

"Yeah, well, don't let the detective hype go to your head. The Harry Books made you famous, and we know who wrote those. I'm your literary father, Harry."

The light went out, plunging Kale into a precarious and frightening blackness.

"Harry, I take it all back. Turn the light on!"

With a chuckle, Harry flicked on the big lamp and lit up the steps allowing Kale to catch up, then he turned and started down at a furious pace. Still breathless from the whack to his sternum, Kale followed thinking the narrow steps endless. His sigh of relief at reaching the bottom echoed a dozen times. Harry turned and lit up the long narrow stairway. Kale figured it was about fifty feet to the top.

Harry moved his light along a solid wall of chiseled slate and back down the other side. "Bit like the Black Hole of Calcutta, innit?"

Kale spread his arms and placed a hand on both walls. "What is this place, Harry? I can barely breathe down here."

"A way out of that Norman tower is my guess. All those old garrisons and castles had emergency exits."

A few hesitant steps forward and the passage veered off sharply to the right and then narrowed considerably. Kale sidled along sideways.

"Hold the light higher, Harry. I think I see something up ahead." A few more shuffling sidesteps and the passage opened into a small room containing empty crates and broken bottles. Kale pointed toward the corner where Harry's light glinted off a shiny garden tool. "Potter's scythe! I saw that in the garden shed at the Priory. Hard to imagine why he'd keep it down here."

Harry sighed. "I would guess, as a weapon."

Empty bean cans lay strewn across the floor, and broken glass scrunched underfoot with every step. Harry sniffed the air like a hound. "Smell anything familiar?"

"Burned wood, like a doused campfire."

"Anything else?"

Kale sniffed the air again. "Raspberry! I smell raspberry."

Flashing his light around, Harry found a kerosene lantern hanging on the wall and lit it. In the brightening glow, Kale discovered the reason for the assortment of digging tools. The entire end of the small room was a solid wall of burned beams and rubble with a small hole at the bottom just large enough for a man to crawl through. Gingerly dropping down on one knee, Harry

explored the tunnel with his lamp inadvertently illumi-
nating the small bits of green glass scattered about the
floor. Kale stooped and picked up a large piece embossed with the Wychwood Spirit brand.

He was elated. "We must be almost under the tower.
Let's try and make it through."

"It could be twenty feet. And remember, Potter was
very small," Harry replied. Another quick peek into the
hole, and he proclaimed it unsafe. "Bloody thing could
collapse at anytime. I suggest we remove ourselves
from here in a hurry."

Kale pushed past him and spied what Harry had
seen. "A skeleton, holding an ancient shovel."

"We're not calling Scotland Yard on this one, Harry
said. "They'll never let us alone at this rate. And that
one's been there since long before our time."

"I'd say about two hundred years. *Down a tunnel
with a key, many bottles filled for thee. Shut the door,
make no sound, spend your life underground.*"

Harry looked at him quizzically.

"A kid's jump-rope rhyme to frighten would-be
thieves. Jenkins recited it to me. Apparently it worked
and no one ever knew."

On the way up, piqued by Harry's lack of bravado,
Kale asked how much money the poker chips had
brought in.

"I don't remember. Ask Neddy," he replied. "But I
think it was enough to start the roof and get rid of that
used-up thing you call a car, and get something more
suitable for country life."

Kale could tell Harry was miffed at his one-upmanship on the jump-rope rhyme.

They found the manor kitchen deserted, only a dripping tap disturbed the quiet. On the counter lay a note in hard, precise handwriting, a Neddy memo: *Tired of waiting. Gone to bed. Be up early!*

"Sleep tight!" Harry said, already headed for the steps. Grabbing a piece of cheddar from the refrigerator, Kale hauled himself into the living room and flopped onto the sorry excuse of a sofa. *I wonder what's to happen to all this furniture. Do we own it?* Turning, he raised his head and eyed the far corner of the darkened room where the collection of lead soldiers stood on silent guard. *The furnishings were never mentioned in the sale; that could be a huge mistake. I suppose Bertie will want his family heirlooms. Too bad, what?* Kale chuckled at his lingua spoofa and let his head drop back onto a cushion. Be nice to find the Cavendish diamond and buy our own furnishings. Where would Mary have hidden it? Did she tell her girls the elixir was slowly making people crazy? Is that why they were killed? Lord Caddington might have killed them while in a drunken stupor? Makes sense, but why do it so brutally? Perhaps the murderer killed the girls one by one to make Mary talk. But talk about what? Where her diamond was hidden? He dismissed that idea immediately; Mary was an ancestor of Tori's. He couldn't imagine either lady holding a large piece of carbon above so many lives.

"Kale? What are you doing here by yourself?" Tori

slipped into the room wearing a dressing gown many sizes too big and made a beeline to the still warm fireplace. She turned to warm her backside. "Well?"

"Oh, just thinking about diamonds and crazy people."

"Diamonds are for dreaming about and there are too many crazies in this world to waste sleep on. You get yourself to bed. I'm going into the kitchen for a glass of milk. You better be gone when I get back."

He watched her slip off into the dark like a sprite, but it wasn't until he heard the kitchen door close that her words struck a chord: *too many crazies.* Maybe someone was still after the elixir recipe.

At first light, a squeaky wheel heralded the arrival of Wheems and his roofing crew. Up early for a jog and wreathed in mist, Kale stood watching the giant as he set his four helpers to hauling scaffold. He watched him walk to his truck and muscle his compact telescoping ladder from the top. "Open the front door," Wheems ordered one of his workmen, and disappeared inside.

Kale moved over a few steps to keep Wheems in view through the open door. He saw the giant walk the entire length of the great hall and place his ladder against the fireplace.

"Now what's he up to?"

A workman closed the door leaving Kale thinking Wheems was probably checking the stability of the chimney stone. Kale strode across to the door and cracked it open for a peek. No sign of Wheems, but Neddy was just coming down the stairs. "Hey Neddy! Keep an eye on that roofer. Tell me if he goes anywhere other than the chimney." Kale waved and jogged away into the cool mist.

The crisp moist air invigorated Kale. He rounded the east wing at a full run. With only a cursory glance at the scene of Potter's demise and last night's sojourn into the depths, he sped north across the acres of dew-sodden meadow toward the ribbon of hill that surrounded the manner like the rim of a soup bowl.

Cresting the rise, he found himself trotting through a spooky mist that obscured all but the nearest of the great oaks. Slow down, he thought. But the hard packed ground seemed made for running fast and, ignoring caution, he poured on the coals and made puffing noises like a steam engine. Feeling unstoppable, he let out a shout of joy and narrowly missed colliding with a huge stone. Winded, he stopped at the next of the gray-white stele Bertie had called Roll Round Stones. Panting, he leaned back against the cool stone and watched a breeze riffle the mist like a wheat field exposing more of the strange stones. Kale had considered them spooky when he saw them from the road, but up close they looked even more like half-buried skulls. His already tripping heart banged in his chest like a hammer. He wanted out of that field, but a step away he froze; something moved in the mist, something coming his way. Ducking back behind the huge stone he held his breath, plastering himself against its cold wetness. He could see them now, a line of hooded, shovel-toting figures moving like the ghosts of lost miners: Druids.

Kale let them get out of sight and followed them down to the river. From behind the trunk of an oak tree, he stood watching them crowd into a small boat and go paddling off into the mist toward the opposite bank. Kale turned to retrace his steps, but a shout from across the river stopped him dead. He knew that voice.

"Abner Snow," Kale said to himself a bit too loudly.

"What was that?" Abner shouted. "Any of you hear somebody call my name?"

"Nah! You've been down in that tunnel too long boss." Then came the sharp report of a hand striking soft flesh. "Ow! You didn't need do that boss. I'll be quiet."

Kale easily backtracked Snow and his mob. He followed the trail through the oaks down into the bowl of pastureland surrounding the manor. The ground mist had thickened and almost prevented him from finding the square of artificial turf. Yanking it back like an old carpet, he exposed a round, dark hole and a shiny aluminum ladder. Kale looked from the hole to the manor and back and remembered Bertie saying the south wing had burned to the ground.

"Trying for a back door, eh, Abner?"

Shoveling in some pebbles with the toe of his sneaker, Kale endured the few seconds of silence with extreme trepidation. "Why me? Why not Harry?" Fifteen rungs down, he smelled burned wood, shepherd's pie, and a big rat named Abner Snow.

Kale hated dark places. He missed the bottom rung. Glass shattered. In the miserable confines of that wet pit, it sounded like a gunshot. Kale ducked down and struck his knee on something hard—a flashlight—a big one of considerable capabilities. When he flicked the switch a powerful beam illuminated not only a rubble-filled tunnel, but portions of the large space beyond. Kneeling down on one knee, he attempted to maneuver the light beam, but to no avail—too much rubbish.

"A person would be a damn fool to go in there," he said aloud, already crawling into the narrow confines of the tunnel.

Kale wasn't halfway to the end when bits of old plaster rained down on him, filling the air with choking dust. Now he couldn't see at all and his heart had jumped into his mouth. Thoughts of being trapped became too much, and he began to crawl backward. Coughing and blinded by dust, he managed to gain the relative security of the pit and collapsed onto his backside. "Whew, now that was close!" He hauled himself onto his feet and started up the ladder. Out of the hole and gulping air like a prairie dog, he carefully replaced the cover of fake grass.

Raindrops struck the back of his neck. "Does it always rain here?" he muttered.

"Wouldn't be Cotswold without rain," called out a cheerful voice.

"Tori!"

Trotting from the mist wearing shorts and a cut-up sweat, she ran in place like a hovering angel. Kale guessed from the raised eyebrow what would come next.

"You look a mess, Kale. You're all dusty."

Knowing she would demand to go down the hole, Kale immediately set off toward the manor while telling her he'd fallen into an ash pit at the Roll Right

Stones. Far enough away he told her of seeing Abner Snow and his digging crew.

"What were they digging?"

"A new back door for the manor."

"You're a silly goose, Kale. C'mon, I'll race you to the front door. It's going to rain all day and I think this is as good a time as any to haul out the laptops and get our outlines down pat."

"A story? You mean you actually have one in mind? What's it about? Mary Gant obviously, but what's the slant?"

"Her life and loves. But you just write your own. Who knows, maybe we'll meet in the middle and pull our chestnuts from the flame of financial ruin together."

Lightning suddenly stabbed into the forest grabbing Kale's full attention. From off in the mist, like a disappearing apparition, Tori yelled back. "It's a sign! Write good, write fast, or the devil will get you!"

Chapter Fifteen

Kale spent the entire next day in his room typing to the rhythm of the omnipresent rain. It ruled every page. "Dribble drivel," he said to himself. Disgusted, he stopped and listened to the ceiling drip water into a dozen cans. *Poink! Poink! Poink!* The hypnotic sound caused his eyes to glaze. No words would come.

Kale gave up, stuck his feet up on the desk and watched the rain lash against the windows. He thought about murder and counted the victims aloud. "Mary's twelve girls, Cassidy in the secret room, the barman in the river, Potter the gardener, and now the old skeleton in the tunnel."

As he listened to the drone of water dripping down from an acre of leaky roof, he absently wondered if Abner and his mob were digging at the rabbit hole.

Kale reached for his laptop, deleted the twenty pages

of soggy nonsense, and began typing *Mary's Story.* He used the infamous rhyme as a lead: *Mary Mary quite contrary, how does your garden grow? With silver bells and cockleshells and pretty maids all in a row.*

"I need inspiration," he said aloud and went to examine the bookshelves. He found a leather-bound dictionary and thinking to examine the binding he pulled it out slowly, wondering if it would open yet another secret door, but it didn't. It was just a well-worn book. Or so he thought until he opened it. The pages inside had been cut away to make room for a smaller book.

"Handwritten. A diary." He sat on the edge of the bed wondering whose life story he had stumbled upon, and if it were something book-worthy, or at least inspiring.

The first gilded page said it all: *Mary Catherine Gant.* He gasped. Could this be a more detailed diary from Mary Gant? He sprawled across the bed and read the first few pages intensly. "Not Mary Gant, Catherine, her niece," he mumbled to himself, disappointed. But then he brightened, "I can tell Mary's story from the niece's perspective." He flipped the page and kept reading, mostly insignificant events in a young girl's life. It seemed Catherine and William had been orphaned and Mary-Mary had secured them positions at the manor, just as Tori had related. He sat up midway, where her writing became tight scrawls.

For days, William hath been raving about some liqueur of M'Lord Caddington's. I can see the gleam of it in his eyes as he talks to me. I do wish he'd put it aside. The raspberry odor weakens my stomach.

A few pages later:

William brought the elixir with him tonight, sure that it will heal my recent ailment. I must admit, I liked it well. It stirred in my head like a wonderful dream and my senses yearn for more.

A knot formed in Kale's stomach as he thought of Jenkins' nursery rhyme about Lord Caddington's traps. Next entry:

M'Lord has sent William from the manor. With heavy heart, he hath gained him station in the stables with Squire Elderby. My dear William, my sole sibling, shunted to the lowest of stable boys. I can't bear it. M'Lord said he brought the situation upon himself and left no recourse. I confess he's not been himself of late. He smells odd and continues to wrought mischief between the other boys with his sharp tongue and short temper. He's been crawling about in the passageways like a lowly rat of late searching for more of the elixir. I yearn for it myself and bid him look for it.

Kale paused. Was the elixir that addictive? One taste had hooked them? Perhaps that was the recipe they'd found in the safe, the hallucinogenic formula made with wormwood. He read on how Catherine accepted William's fate, though slow to recover until some weeks later when a visitor came calling.

Master Roche, my aunt's coachman called to-day with a message from Aunt Mary to M'Lady. M'Lady sent him to the kitchen for tea while she prepared her reply. M'Lady bade me serve him. Too bold, he compared my eyes to the midnight sky. I shan't have the nerve to speak to him, yet my heart dreams of him returning with yet another message from my dearest aunt. Oh, how I flush with feelings more glorious than those wrought by the elixir that exiled poor William.

Kale laughed aloud. "Oh, Tori, if only you were as easy to win over as Catherine. I'll have to try the original Mr. Roche's line out on you: "Your eyes shine like the midnight sky.""

The romance progressed with sporadic entries, but the diary took a dramatic turn again:

William returned tonight through the passage-way. He seems determined to find M'Lord's secret cache of elixir. Poor William speaks nonsense about the elixir being his just due, and Mary's di-amond his inheritance, though Aunt Mary told me herself it belongs not to her. She told me she holds it on loan. By what means would a nun have such a possession? William babbles on in rhymes. I fail to understand him anymore.

Kale grimaced. No doubt the boy had gotten hold of the original wormwood version with its mind-altering formula. The next entry was similar:

> *Three times William hath returned, each time worse than before, not like my dear William at all. He raves and quotes strange poetry. He claims to have found a passage to the cellars. He only needs the key. He charges me to find it, with threat of harm if I don't. And he hath gone mad for the procession of Aunt Mary's diamond. He hath urged me to ask Aunt Mary for it. What right or use does a nun have of such a jewel, he asks. There is a girl he fancies, one of high station who won't look at him in the stables. He wants the diamond to purchase a new life. He hath gone crazy with his notions. Perhaps M'Lord was right to send William away. I shall have to confess to M'Lord of his coming to my rooms at night. He frightens me.*

Kale drummed his fingers on the bed. So, William had his eyes on an upper-class girl, got himself drunk over it on a bottle of elixir, and became addicted. Meanwhile, he decides Mary's diamond is the ticket to pull himself out of his lowly life as a stable boy. And he's looking for the key, like in Jenkins' jump-rope rhyme. Kale imagined the heated discussion between the boy and Mary.

> *Aunt Mary paid a visit today. She said she had to deposit an important paper with the monks of Medlenham, something that had fraught great*

*harm she hadn't foreseen. She'll be gone a fort-
night and bade me stay close to the manor, as if I
ever leave. She inquired after William and watched
my expression for an answer. I did naught but cry
and say William had become quite ill. She bade me
keep him in line. "Someone's been about Lord
Caddington's liqueurs, and traps have been set,"
she said.*

Kale frowned. The traps. Perhaps that's what Cassidy had been caught in, one of Caddington's traps. Is it
possible the trap lay dormant two hundred years and
caught the wrong prey? The empty bottles must have
been some of the elixir, set out like cheese for a mouse.
But William hadn't ever found them, Cassidy did. Then
he thought of the skeleton in the tunnel—William.

Mary's dialogue continued in the diary:

*Aunt Mary told me more. "My influence over
Lord Caddington is not as strong as the devil I
plied from the garden and trapped in a bottle."
Aunt Mary stirred my soul with the directness of
her eyes, but I only looked at the chain about her
neck. Her whistle no longer shared a space with
the diamond. "Your diamond!" I exclaimed, and
she replied, "If it were a needle in a haystack, only
those that eat hay shall find it."*

Kale gasped. "So Mary did hide it! Some imagery,"
he mumbled. "It's not a needle in a haystack, it's a diamond among liquor bottles, so only those who drink

liquor will find it," he concluded. "It must be hidden here at the manor, in the cellar with the private stash." Heart pounding, he continued to read and found a note tucked into the next page, in Mary's handwritting.

"You must keep William from quenching his thirst, sweet Catherine. I go now to request help from the monks. Perhaps they will help William to wash the devil from his soul."

Kale read the note again. Mary must have realized what the elixir was doing to William and knew the damage the recipe could do if it fell into the wrong hands, so she placed it with the monks for safekeeping. That's how it had ended up in the monks' files, and it had stayed there until his old boss Enoch Tulley had come across it. Tulley swiped it from the Monks and placed it in the Galley Press Safe.

Next entry:

William is mad to find the passage to the elixir. He says Mary has run from him in fear and believes not that she has gone to visit the monastery. He claims she hath no reason to visit monks. Tonight William said Aunt Mary is not our aunt at all, but our mother. Impossible. Aunt Mary is a sister of the cloth, and well respected. My hand refuses to relate the name William put to Aunt Mary, but he implies we are her bastard children. He claims all the sisters of the church are . . . oh, I

*dare not repeat it. He will go to them and secure
his own supply of elixir, and Mary's girls shall go
to the devil.*

*I wish Aunt Mary would return. How hath my
brother—he comes again—*

The last entry was scrawled hurriedly:

*Great doom hath come upon the town. Where is
William? I fear to say what's in my heart. I dare
not even write it here. Master Roche awaits me.
M'Lord has granted him my hand and given leave
for him to carry me away from Wychwood.*

The remaining pages were blank. Kale flopped back
and stared at the ceiling, listening to the drum of rain.
So, William, half-crazy from the elixir, murdered the
girls. Mary had already escaped with the recipe to put it
under lock and key in the monastery, and perhaps beg
the monks' help in saving William. Or so one would
suppose from the entries. There was still no conclusion
to be made about Mary's disappearance, but William?
Since the authorities never executed anyone for the
murders, William must be the corpse in the tunnel, the
second victim of Lord Caddington's traps.

He would have to tell Tori, but not yet. It would be
hard news to hear that Mary's son, Tori's ancestral uncle, was the mad murderer.

He held the book in his hands, thinking. Maybe there
was a clue there, but he couldn't figure out what it might

be. He shoved it back among the others and made up his mind he'd burn the whole musty lot of them, clean up the shelves, and let Tori have the room. It was fitting.

Then he sat down at his laptop and began to write William's story, except in Kale's version William would be a hero trying to save the women. He wrote until the sun had dipped behind the great oaks of the forest, painting his room with tiny splashes of color.

Stretching aching limbs, Kale picked up the binoculars and stood in the window to watch the departing barn workers speed up a lane freshly studded with new fence posts. He made sure Hermes Wheems was among them before lowering the binoculars and returning to the business at hand.

He was thirty pages into *Mary's Story* and knew he had a gripping tale that would be in the bookshops by Christmas. All it needed was financing, which brought him back to the diamond. Did William ever get his hands on it? Catherine had said William had been crawling around the passages like a rat. Were there more passages? Perhaps he had found another way to the cellar? Mulling over Potter's last words, he browsed the bookshelves. What had he meant by horse buns? Kale stopped and contemplated a moldy first edition of Sherlock Holmes. He'd read all of Conan Doyle's books and remembered a line of advice given to Doctor Watson by the ineludible Holmes: *Eliminate all the impossible, and you're left with the only possible solution.*

Eliminate the impossible? Kale felt compelled to take the words at face value. Harry was right; a man isn't likely to spit out nonsense on death's doorstep.

Potter must have meant . . . an image suddenly blasted into his gray matter like an F16 fighter plane. "The stuffed horse in the armory!" He felt stupid not to have seen it before. "That's the key!"

Chapter Sixteen

Kale descended the hidden spiral stairs in record time, burst from Tori's bathroom, and threw himself into an overstuffed chair. "I figured it out. I know what the gardener meant by 'horse buns.' "

Unflappable, Tori kept on with her stacking of books into nooks and crannies. "Come to watch me suffer, have you?"

Kale rolled his eyes. "Listen to me, I'm serious now." Her momentary attention garnered, he explained his stuffed horse theory. "Bertie said he pounded the floor everywhere, but I'll bet he missed the floor under that horse. It's the only thing that makes any sense—the only possible connection to horse buns."

Momentarily lost in thought, Tori suddenly flung away her armload of books and jumped in the air. "You're right!" Her face lit up like a sunrise on the ocean—but then her demeanor slowly collapsed. "We're not very good at treasure hunting, are we? We should have made that connection."

"Phooey! We found the stash under the hotel."

"Yes, but—"

"No buts. We're doing great. Now let's go see what's under that horse."

"Well, maybe you're right." Smiling now, she walked briskly to her desk, saved her documents, shut down her computer and slipped shoes onto her feet. "I'm ready. Let's go find that diamond."

"I'll ask Neddy to bring a bucket of soapy water. If there's an opening it will be hidden by dirt. We'll pour the water on the floor and see if it goes anywhere, like in the church. Oh, and I saw two crowbars in the mudroom off the kitchen. I'll get those, you find something to mark the floor."

"Crowbars? Oh, you mean pry bars, the things housewreckers use. There's some chalk in the kitchen."

They found Harry in the kitchen and dragged him to the tower still munching a sandwich. A confused Neddy followed, lugging a bucket of soapy water.

In the tower like a cleaning crew, Harry and Kale had a go at moving the horse and retired red-faced from exertion. "How did those horses manage with all that heavy armor?"

Harry pointed down at the rectangular base, "It's this here, innit? It's just four squared off oak timbers. Thing weighs a ton."

Off to one side, Neddy stood ready with her bucket.

"Dump water, watch it ebb away. It's an old trick."

Tori stood at the ready with a piece of chalk to mark

the waters egress. "Come on, Harrykins. Heave at it one more time. Kale, use those muscles."

Harry grimaced, and bending low at the waist, stepped over the oak base and under the horse's belly. He took a deep breath, spit on both hands and lifted.

"It's off the ground," Kale yelled. Pushing with all his might, he slid the great animal forward. Behind him, Neddy emptied her bucket of water with a cry of pure glee.

Ready with the chalk, Tori moved in quickly, but instead of marking the tiles she turned and looked up at Kale. "We've been beat to the punch." She pointed to a faintly defined outline of a trapdoor.

Neddy chuckled, "I told you it's an old trick."

Kale dropped to a knee for a closer look, frowned at the outline, and told Harry about Abner Snow working on digging a tunnel in from the outside.

Harry looked livid. "You should have told me all this earlier. I'm going to kill that man!" With a growl, Harry grabbed up a crowbar and attacked the trap door. It wouldn't budge, not even with Kale straining on the other bar.

Frustrated, Harry tossed away the iron bar making a great echoing racket. "Well, there is a bright side. Whoever beat us to finding this door didn't have any better luck. We have to find another way. We'll have to try Abner's rat hole, and if I find him there, I'll make him rue the day he was born."

Neddy patted his back. "Calm down. Kale told you that tunnel is too dangerous. Why don't you just call in the police and report trespassers?"

"We can't do that, Neddy," Tori said. "They'll twig to our shenanigans at the hotel and we'll lose everything to Inland Revenue. We—"

Neddy threw up her hands, "I don't want to know! That way I won't have to lie at your trials. Well, if we can't call in the police, let's go check out the chimney."

Harry looked amused. "Why should we do that?"

"Well, Kale asked me to keep an eye on that roofer, so after I finished setting up a Galley Press reception desk in the hall, I sat and watched the brute go up and down the chimney like a monkey. Whoever heard of taking equipment up to a roof through the chimney? And he took up scads. I've been thinking there's something up there, perhaps a ventilation shaft."

Kale looked outraged. "Why didn't you tell me?"

"He didn't go anywhere but the chimney. You said—"

"Yes, yes, I know. My fault."

Harry stared at her. Kale could almost hear the gears working. The old Norman keep got so quiet Kale could hear a dripping sound coming from way down below their feet; Poink! Poink! Poink!

Harry moved so fast it surprised Neddy into dropping her bucket. With a swoop of his hand he grabbed up a crowbar and headed for the short hallway connecting the armory to the great hall. Neddy and Tori both squealed with delight and galloped after him, leaving Kale to search for the second crowbar. "Pry bar," he said to himself, laughing at the echo. By the time he'd located the bar and loped across to the great hall, Harry had started up the ladder like a Russian circus bear.

Seconds passed, then along with a shower of soot came a plaintive cry, "Help me. I'm stuck!"

Leaning on the ladder rungs, Neddy hollered back, "Keep moving, Harry. I'm setting a big fire in the hearth." She stood back and whispered to Kale, "I'm claustrophobic. You go."

Muttering under his breath, Kale climbed up to the bulbous blockage and pulled.

"Not down! Up," Harry cried. "Just a few more inches; there's a passage here. Push!"

Annoyed, Kale braced his back against the rough stone and shoved his stocky friend up the soot-blackened chimney like a bottlebrush.

After a few heavy gasps and a string of complaints about the soot, Harry called for another electric torch. "A big one!"

"There are some in the kitchen. I'll get them," Neddy yelled back.

Kale went down for the light, but when he climbed back, there was no sign of Harry, just three narrow, square passages, heating ducts. "Harry! Where are you, Harry?" No answer. When he turned to holler down to Tori, two heads suddenly popped into view an arm's length away, both looking wide-eyed and breathless.

"Wheems! He's coming," Tori gasped. "The squeaky wheel, we heard it coming down the lane. What do we do now?"

Kale knew exactly what to do . . . turn up the volume. "Harr-eeee!"

Harry's muffled instructions sounded very far away.

"Don't panic, it's the passage on your right. Just pull the ladder up and bring it here."

"Easy for him to say. I don't think it'll fit," Kale muttered.

With help from the ladies he put his back into the task and began pulling up the ladder rung by rung, telescoping the ladder into a bendable size. Getting it up and into the narrow passage wasted precious minutes. Panting from the exertion, the three headed down the narrow passage—an old slate heat duct used to spread heat from the fireplace to the upper rooms.

"It's beginning to curve and go up," Tori whispered. "We're in the walls of the Norman tower. Central heating, amazing!"

Harry hissed at them in the dark, "You sure took your sweet time."

Kale aimed the beam of his flashlight toward the voice. "Getting this ladder in here was like pulling a square peg through a round hole, Harry."

Working a crowbar between loose stones, Harry glanced up into the beams of light. "Good show. Now, put it down and come help."

"What are you doing?"

"Making a hole through to the cellar, of course. Remember the water drip? If we can bust through this floor, we ought to have access to the cellar below."

"How can you be sure?"

"That architect explained it, remember? He told us how the Normans quarried the rock and built right over the quarries, so this place must have a quarry under it— and that's our cellar."

Kale dropped his end of the burden. The loud clank caused Neddy to utter a small scream. Tori's protective arm went around Neddy's shoulder. "Harry, tell her we're going to be all right. Tell her we're not going to die in here."

Harry looked over and shrugged, "There's a good chance of that happening. Wheems is a psychopath and undoubtedly has another ladder in his truck. I suggest we all pipe down and get to work. These stones have been worked on for some time, and with a little concentrated effort, we can get them loosed and be down there before he arrives. He's not coming through the front door—it's locked, so whatever time it takes him to get in by whatever means is all the time we have."

Point well taken, Kale thought. The stone Harry had been pulling suddenly fell away, taking along two more for company. Silence hung. When the crash came, it sounded very far away.

"Th-th-that sounds all the way from next week," Neddy said in a voice verging on hysteria.

Kale leaned over, stuck his flashlight down the hole and lit up a vertical shaft that seemed endless. "Harry," he whispered, "that ladder is way too short."

Undaunted by such trifles, Harry turned and began rooting about in Wheems' supplies. From the pile he selected a coil of hefty rope, and got to work constructing a rudimentary ladder.

Kale looked on, impressed.

Harry glanced up and smiled, "It's why I'm the cop, and you're the publisher. When I finish we'll tie this to the ladder and lower away. It should reach the ground."

Harry was right again; the ladder clanked onto the cellar floor and hung there like a Hindu rope trick. They stood ready, but due to an attack of something resembling rigor mortis, Neddy was not going down the ladder. "I can't! My hands, my feet, they won't move."

Harry speedily hunted up another rope, tied it to her waist and lifted her off the floor like a wooden Indian. With Kale helping, they got her poised over the hole and lowered her down to the end of her rope. In the beam of Tori's lamp Neddy swung in and out of view like a clock pendulum—time was running out.

"Well, she's only a few feet short of the bottom. Be a good lad, Kale, pick her up on the way down."

Kale might have resisted being next, but the sooty black confines suddenly echoed with loud angry curses. "Wheems!" Quickly he grabbed Tori and urged her feet onto the rope ladder.

"All set? Then let's go!" He gave her a shove and prepared to launch himself, but stopped short when he heard Harry say, "Kale, wait! Look at this! A portable gas generator."

Kale turned and watched it come with a long string of lamps. He didn't miss a beat; in seconds he had the machine by its long cord and lowered it away. He got it to the ground when the nightmare appeared.

"What are you doing here?" The giant's voice boomed out so loud it sent soot drifting down from the low ceiling.

Kale, who had never actually heard Wheems speak, didn't like the tone one bit.

"Answer me!"

"This is our home, Mr. Wheems," Harry said calmly moving between the stooped-over giant and his pile of supplies.

"I be here first," Wheems growled, advancing on Harry.

"Take it easy," Harry advised, and, slowly easing the pistol from his pocket, leveled it at the monster's mid-section and motioned to Kale. "Quickly now, get to the ladder."

"Harry!"

"Go! I'll be right behind."

Wheems suddenly let out a blood-curdling snarl and charged.

Sensing Harry wouldn't shoot, the monster grabbed Harry with his gorilla arms and began to squeeze. One hand on the rope and leaning into empty space, Kale used up precious seconds getting back on solid footing. Picking up a crowbar he clamored up behind Wheems, heaved it like a baseball bat and struck a homer into center field. The giant released Harry, turned toward Kale, and dropped to the floor like a slaughtered cow.

"What kept you?" Harry gasped, and with only a pause to fill his lungs, hustled them both to the ladder. Kale kept looking back at the fallen giant hoping for a sign of life.

"He's not dead," Harry said. "It would take more then a whack on the head to kill that monster."

Kale wasted no time climbing down and only slowed to gather in the petrified Neddy. "You'll be all right now, Ned. Just a few more feet."

"Frying pan to the fire," she croaked.

Tori stood at the bottom anchoring the ladder and looking pale and distraught and ready to comfort Neddy. "Kale, what happened up there?"

"Wheems. I had to hit him, but I don't think anything will keep him down long. If we don't get that ladder down we'll be in real trouble. Will you look at the size of this cellar! It's like Grand Central Station."

Pulling Harry down the last few rungs, Tori demanded he hand over his knife. "I'll climb up and cut the ladder loose."

"Is there no other way?" Harry said, looking at Kale.

Desperately trying to think of one, Kale could only shrug and grab hold of the ladder.

"Help him, Harry! Neddy, hold a light on me," she yelled, already halfway up.

Tori clambered up the remaining rungs and had the ladder loosened in two shakes of a clasp knife. She looked down grinning and Kale motioned her to hurry—the ladder was too long and skinny to hold.

Tori let loose a blood-chilling scream.

"Wheems!" Kale shouted. "He's got her! Hang onto the ladder, Harry."

Chapter Seventeen

Kale went up the ladder like a circus monkey in his rush to reach Tori. "Let her go!"

Hanging through the shaft and lit up by Neddy's quivering light, the giant's grin looked nightmarish as he began to swing Tori back and forth.

"Let her go," Kale repeated in his most threatening voice.

Wheems gave Tori one final swing . . . and let go.

Instinctively, without a thought for his own safety, Kale hooked a toe under a rung and made a desperate grab. "Gotcha!"

"My hair!' Tori screamed.

Down below, Harry cursed a blue streak as the acrobat reeled in his struggling catch.

"Don't look down, Tori," Kale ordered. "Just grab hold of the rails and slide . . . like a sailor."

Kale thought she did it quite well, in spite of landing

on Harry. Then Kale landed squarely on her. He wrapped her in his arms and rolled them away from the falling ladder. The crowbar followed, struck the stone floor by their heads, and bounced twice. Other assorted digging gear began to rain down.

"Harry! Get Neddy under a table. Quick!"

From the small ventilation shaft high above the cellar floor, Wheems' flashlight cut through the dark revealing a wonderland of carved slate. Kale completely forgot about the danger and watched the light travel along soaring columns, cooking pits, long tables, benches, and a great square depression he could only guess was a bath. The place begged to be explored, and Wheems had temporarily ceased his bombardment of tools. Only, having narrowly missed death from the lunatic's shower of odds and ends, Kale and Tori were not budging from the shelter of the workbench.

"Hearts of oak," he paraphrased, giving the bench a testing thump, "ought to protect us from anything. Everybody okay? Neddy? Harry?"

"We're over on your right Kale, under a bench," Harry yelled.

"Harry?"

"Yes?"

"We're in a bind here."

"Bit of a pickle, but I think he'll soon run out of ammunition."

A long silence ensued wherein even Wheems stopped exploring with his light.

"Harry?"

"Yes?"

"That special recipe was an elixir, a drug. It was addictive and made men go mad. You know that, don't you?"

"The thought's occurred to me."

"I'm thinking maybe Wheems might be privy to a good store of it."

"My thoughts exactly. A mad dog guarding his bone."

"Any idea how we're going to get out of here?"

"By using our wits, and a bit of patience."

Wheems must have been listening because he suddenly plunged the space into darkness. No matter, Harry had a flashlight and the light tour continued. He even supplied commentary. "Big, innit. The Normans must have lived here while they built their tower."

Accompanied by great banging and clunking noises, the threat from above returned with a more powerful lamp. Suspended on Harry's rope ladder, and laughing like a maniacal gorilla, Wheems zeroed onto his targets like he had radar.

"He can see our tracks in the dust," Tori whispered and snuggled closer. "Thank you for what you did on that ladder, Kale. That was very brave of you."

Feeling like Indiana Jones in a tight spot, he pulled her close and she responded with a fervor that surpassed his wildest expectations. A few seconds into a kiss that held much promise, something extra heavy smashed into a nearby table sending Neddy into a screaming fit.

A stubby shadow suddenly leaped up from under a table. Harry, and he stood there in the pool of light cast by Wheems' lamp. Kale watched him raise an arm like he was about to recite something from Shakespeare.

Kale saw the glint of metal. "Harry's got his gun," he whispered, and thought only Harry Bass would have the foresight to hang onto that pistol while Wheems had squeezed him like toothpaste.

Harry fired. The sound exploded in Kale's brain. He covered his ears before the next shot. Then he removed his hands quickly so as not to miss the sound of the ricocheting bullet and the howls of protest coming from Wheems. Harry's third shot turned the monster's big lamp into a shower of sparks and falling glass. The next ricocheted twice and hit its mark. The scream raised the hairs on Kale's neck, but the faint thumping sound of running feet brought a smile. The monster was in full retreat and making a beeline for the chimney.

Out from under the protection of his table, Kale searched the floor for a light. Finding one, he returned to get Tori onto her feet, just as the monster let out with another howl, fainter this time, and slowly diminishing in volume. A great cloud of soot filtered down from the ventilation shaft, like dust through a sunbeam.

"He must have fallen down the chimney. He probably broke his neck," Kale said.

"I hope so," Neddy yelled.

Tori lost no time in maneuvering the generator into place. "Nothing to it, really. My dad loved camping. Ours was just like this one." She grabbed the end of the twenty-bulb string of lights, made a beeline for the row of white-topped stone tables standing guard in the center of the huge room and came running back. Looking at Kale, she leaned over the generator and threw a switch. The machine sprang to life with a loud whine and lit the place like an amusement park. Kale stood blinking, not believing his eyes.

Three wide steps topped with carved pillars ringed the huge oblong-shaped room like a picture frame. Beyond the pillars a walk around fronted heavy iron-strapped oak doors, dozens of them, each centered between pillars. Kale strode forward, tripped, and saved himself from a nasty spill by grabbing hold of a pillar. "Watch the cracks in the steps. And check out these pillars, they're actually carved from the living rock! Those old Normans must have had a lot of time on their hands."

"What is living rock?" Neddy asked.

Glad to see her back in good form, Kale smiled and pointed toward the ceiling. "After quarrying stone for the tower they chipped their way in here and began carving space like Michelangelo. They did a good job too. This place should be a museum."

Harry trotted up and laid an ear against the pillar. "It is live rock. I can hear people walking."

Dubious, Kale put an ear to the pillar, "You're right. It must be coming from the pasture tunnel, Abner's rabbit hole."

"No doubt. Listen up old son, I think we'd better hurry and prepare a little surprise for our friend Abner."

Harry jogged up the three wide stairs and muscled open the first of the long round of doors. Brushing aside cobwebs, he lit the room with his big lamp, and when Kale added his, their combined wattage revealed a large cave room dotted with dozens of raised mounds.

"Barracks. Those are beds."

The next door opened into a macabre scene of cobweb-draped rusted armor. "The armory. Look at all the rusted junk," Harry said, batting away the cobwebs. "Be worth a fortune if it wasn't all ruined."

They went door-to-door bashing open dozens before finding one with a wet floor. "This is it, Kale. That's the water we dumped. This way up to the Norman tower."

Kale stuck his head through the door behind Harry and almost dropped his light at the sight of the great empty space. It reminded Kale of an empty silo, only bigger. Looking at the stairway sent a chill up his spine. Just stones jutting out from the wall in a corkscrew fashion all the way to the top.

Harry traced its winding path with his light. "See, it runs up to that trapdoor under the armored horse. This is our escape route." Leaving the door open, Harry went off to check the remaining rooms by himself.

Tori and Neddy joined Kale in staring up at the very top of the winding stairway. He played his light beam on a huge, round stone attached to a rusty chain. "A counterweight. No wonder we couldn't get that trapdoor open. It must weigh a ton."

Tori nodded. "If the old Normans got overrun or burned, they just pulled themselves down here like turtles. Rather smart chaps, but I wonder how they got out?"

"They had a way," Kale said. He quickly explained

the exit he and Harry had found on the outside, where Potter the gardener had met his death.

"Is there anything else you haven't told us?"

From somewhere down the walkabout, Harry whistled. Kale thought that odd, and exchanged concerned looks with the women. They found him in a room eight doors down perched on a huge pile of crates. "Welcome to Prioress Mary Gant's and Lord Caddington's main liquor depository."

Kale grimaced and thought of the diary. This must have been the stash William was searching for. "Harry, we can't bother with this now. We have to think of something to head off Abner Snow, or we get our butts out of here and call the police. Abner is crazy enough to kill for this stuff."

"Here, here," Neddy concurred.

"Relax. His tunnel will dead-end into stone. Potter drank himself silly on what he found left in the tunnel room and never figured out how to get into this section. Neither did that fellow that's been sitting in there for the past couple of centuries."

"Another dead body?" asked Tori.

"Yes, I found him yesterday. Someone locked the bloke in."

"What?" Tori asked.

Kale shook his head. William's story could wait. "What about Abner's tunnel? It's bound to be headed in the same direction."

"Relax. Grab a bottle. Have a few swigs while we wait for Mr. Snow."

Tori laughed, said something about the Bertillon

family spitting in the eye of Cromwell. Chuckling, she sidled off toward a stack of crates bearing a large, inked picture of a raspberry.

"Don't, Tori."

"Nonsense. My ancestor made it, didn't she?"

"And died for it too."

Tori ignored him. Hoisting a crate upright, she yanked off the top and tugged at a bottle. "Looks promising, this one. These bottles were stored on their sides just like those under the hotel. But perhaps not all—this bottle is stuck!" She pulled harder, this time the bottle came out easily, sending her sprawling backward. The bottle smashed against the wall.

The foursome froze. Kale's heart pounded in his ears. He felt sure the noise would give them away to Abner Snow. "He must be through the rabbit hole. He can't be far away," Kale whispered.

A long silence ensued, one finally broken by a faint pounding from the depths of the huge room. Kale quietly eased over to Tori and hauled her up off the floor. "You okay?"

"I'm fine. Is that your rabbit hole he's coming through?"

Kale nodded. He felt sick thinking he could have destroyed it before now.

Harry put a finger across his lips, took Neddy by the hand, and disappeared down a row. Kale and Tori followed behind counting crates. "There must be a thousand cases in here," he whispered.

"Enough to make the manor new again," Tori whispered back.

"Or a new office building—in London," Neddy added.

"Quiet," Harry whispered and shone his light down the wall and onto a small depression filled with sand. He pointed to his ear and then to the wall.

Leaning forward they all put an ear to the cold slate and listened to Abner Snow say, "Quiet! Do you hear something?"

One of his goons replied, "I don't hear nuthin', boss. You sure that old gardener said the bottles were on the other side of this wall? No hole anywhere."

"Yes, I'm sure. Now put your ears to the wall and listen. I heard something, I'm sure I did. Oh, and one of you get that stick of dynamite fused, we're going to blow this wall."

Kale gasped. Only a fool would set off dynamite in an enclosed area, a thought shared by Harry. "The bloody fools will kill themselves," he whispered, putting a finger over his pursed lips to indicate quiet, he motioned to Kale to pull the ladies away from the wall. After making sure all ears were away from the slate, Harry slowly drew his gun and tapped the wall with its stubby barrel. The desired response was quick in coming and heard clearly.

"I heard it, boss! A tapping noise! Here, put your ear to the wall, you can hear it."

Bang! Bang! Harry fired into the wall twice blowing slate like shrapnel. Pain coursed from Kale's eardrums, Neddy sobbed uncontrollably, and Tori took a swing at Harry, cursing him like an alley bum.

Kale's hearing returned enough for him to hear the

slate wall still ringing like a bell. Another few seconds and his numbed auditory nerves had recovered enough to hear the piercing screams from beyond the ringing wall. Screams soon followed by the heavy stomp of boots as Abner and his men fled down the rabbit hole.

On the way back to the door and its blessed light, Kale mulled over the thought that Harry had just saved Abner Snow's bacon. "Good for you, Harry," he said, and would have moved to pat the hero's back if a sudden cry hadn't stopped his heart.

"WHEEEEEEEMS!" Neddy screamed.

Covered head to toe in black soot, the monster loomed in the doorway like a giant tar baby. Neddy had been right; he had fallen down the chimney. How could he have survived such a fall after being shot? With a roar he tottered into the room like Frankenstein's monster and headed straight for the open case of Mary's elixir. "Mine!"

Kale backed against the wall, pulling Tori with him.

Wheems slowly drew out a long knife, hacked off the top of a bottle and threw back the entire contents. Dropping the bottle, he belched like a foghorn and froze there, not moving, paralyzed.

Minutes passed in absolute silence, then ignoring his companion's whispered warnings, Kale approached the monster in the manner of a hunter walking up on a wounded animal. "Wheems? Can you hear me?"

The giant didn't move, he just stood staring at nothing. No response. Kale passed his hand in front of the monster's eyes. Nothing. Glancing over his shoulder at his companions, he said, "The man's dead on his feet."

The others crawled out of hiding and eased around the monstrous man. He blinked.

"He's not dead!" Neddy cried and they all ran for the escape hatch up to the armored horse in the Norman keep.

The way out seemed simple enough; just ascend the silo steps, push the round boulder off the top, and let the law of gravity take over. In a matter of minutes, they should be standing in the manor armory.

Holding both a crate of Mary's goods and a flashlight, Harry gave the steps a few test jumps before starting his winding way to the top. Carrying a crowbar, Neddy followed close on his heels, then Tori and Kale. Steep and wide, the steps wound around and around and made Kale feel like a fly on a wall.

They didn't notice the growing light at the bottom as the silo door slowly swung open.

Bright light and a blood curdling wail filled the silo at precisely the same moment Harry put his foot on the ballast stone. "Mine! Mine!"

Neddy went ballistic. "Wheeeeeeeeeems!"

Tori pushed Neddy upward. "The guy has more lives then a cat. Look! He's gone and dragged in the lamps from the generator. What is he doing down there?"

Like a star in some demented stage show, Wheems started up an Indian war dance complete with whoops and dodge-em's.

"Putting on a show, looks like," Harry said.

The lunatic suddenly stopped his bouncing and made

a threatening gesture with the tool from Potter's tunnel—the scythe.

"Oh, no, he's coming!"

Kale wasn't too concerned; Harry had his gun and Wheems climbed stairs with the speed and alacrity of a sloth.

Tori played Harry's flashlight beam along the rusty chain of the counterbalance. "I don't like the looks of that," she said, indicating the spot where the chain entered the pulley mechanism. "I don't think it will hold. It's probably why the stone is sitting on the step. One would expect a counterbalance to be hanging. Wouldn't one? I think, we should go down and find Abner's rabbit hole."

"Wheems has Potter's scythe," Kale reminded her.

"Do something," Neddy squeaked. "Quick!"

Kale looked over and his heart jumped two beats. Bounding up the steps two and three at a time, Wheems looked like the grim reaper running the Olympic hurdles. Still not too concerned, he called up to Harry. "Better get your pistol ready."

"Stop interrupting. Can't you see I'm busy with this rock? There are no bullets left in the gun. Think of something else."

A beseeching look at Tori received only a raised eyebrow as she stepped up closer to Harry.

"Think of something," Neddy wailed.

Left to his only resource, Kale yanked the top from the case of Mary's elixir and withdrew a bottle. Hefting it a few times he tried to imagine himself back on the

Yale pitcher's mound waiting out a Harvard lad edging off third base. He aimed and threw hard. The bottle flew end over end and caught Hermes Wheems right between the eyes.

"Bull's-eye," Neddy yelled.

Wheems shook his head, dropped the scythe, and wobbled back down the corkscrew stair leaving a trail of bloody brandy.

Tori snatched a bottle from the crate. "This will settle my nerves very nicely, thank you."

"Better not, Tori," Kale said. "I'm pretty sure that's the bad stuff."

Tori uncorked a bottle and took four nerve-calming gulps before moving up a step. But there she hesitated, smelling something . . . smoke.

Down below, Hermes Wheems had again taken centerstage, this time with a fire. Dancing, jumping, and weaving about his little fire, he looked even more energetic. He waved, and ducked out the door for more brandy crates to feed his flames. Brandy made for a substantial blaze.

Harry picked up his crowbar and started on the rock like a Siberian quartz miner.

"It's moving! The rock is moving," Tori shouted. "Keep at it!"

"Faster!" Neddy yelled. "He's throwing more crates on the fire. Hurry!"

"Get up here and push, Kale!" Harry yelled.

Kale put all his strength into one great shove.

"Kale! Be careful!" Tori reached out an arm and reeled him in from the edge. "Hope I'm wrong about that chain," she said, slamming him hard against the wall.

The boulder dropped to the end of a dozen feet of rusty chain and stopped dead. Quivering like a plucked guitar string, the chain jerked once, twice, and began to feed itself into the pulley mechanism.

Elated, Kale shouted, "The trapdoor! It's opening!"

In a roaring avalanche of dust, rock, and rusty parts, the huge stone counterweight broke loose and sailed down like a bomb. Expecting the worst, Kale threw Tori into the wall and yelled, "Hang on!"

Ka-boom . . .

The tower lurched like a giant cannon. Stone, glass, metal, and assorted stuff ricocheted around making noise like a rocket engine. Something soft smacked into the wall by Kale's head—a Wellie boot. Kale wanted to grab it, but had to hang on when the stair he and Tori shared began to shake like a leaf. Looking down over his shoulder he saw the cause, the great ballast stone had bounced like an Indian rubber ball. The stone bounced again and shot out the open door. Then something whizzed past his face, and for a nanosecond he was eye-to-eye with the head of the armored horse. A strange thought flitted through his mind, some whisper about the horse as he wondered what happened to the rest of the body.

Grabbing his arm, Tori screamed, "Climb!"

In seconds the four had scrambled up the few remaining stairs and were climbing through the gaping hole in the armory floor. Kale popped up behind the rest, and in the darkness of the Norman keep, ran straight into Tori.

Harry paused, listening. "It's Abner. I hear his voice." And off he streaked, headed for the great hall.

Kale recited a quick prayer and peeked down into the hole. It looked quiet enough. He headed for the light switch only to find it dangling in pieces.

"Kale," Tori hissed from the dark, and he saw her shadow flit past the armored horse. On its side, broken and headless, the once proud horse looked like a very bad omen.

Kale stepped across to the racks of crossbows and selected one he thought serviceable. Holding his breath, he cranked the bow taut and slipped in the bolt. He turned, armed, but certainly not ready for the sight of Tori running barefoot, the bottle of elixir still in her hand.

"Wait for me!"

Chapter Eighteen

Harry's shout sounded distorted by the roar of the rushing river. "Grab a torch! We've got to catch Abner's goons!"

Running with the heavy bow in hand spent Kale's strength. He stopped, gasping for air like a drowning man. The wind and rain had stopped and the smell of honeysuckle perfumed the soft night air. He stared at the huge white of the moon busting through a break in the storm clouds.

A scream cut through his kaleidoscope vision like a sharp knife. "Tori!" Not sure what direction the scream had come from, he stepped out and waited.

No more screams, only a war-whoop from Harry as he exploded out from the trees swinging a big stick. Kale watched him charge the riverbank like a battle-maddened warhorse. Kale happily joined in the fray and galloped pell-mell in the same direction. The

Charge of the Light Brigade all over again, Kale thought, and for one precious minute he imagined himself astride a huge, panting warhorse swinging a brass-handled sword and bearing down on the enemy lines—presuming Harry had Abner's goons in sight.

Suddenly Abner appeared from behind, snatched the bow from Kale's hands and made off like a bandit toward Wheems who was lumbering like a mad baboon toward the river. Too late, he saw Tori standing with the now half-empty bottle of elixir still in hand, twirling and dancing and singing at the top of her lungs. She was directly in Wheems's path.

Wheems picked her up like a rag doll and tossed her into a waiting boat. With one push of a pole, the boat was swept into the raging waters.

The twang of the bow combined with Tori's scream of rage made the scene seem surreal. By the iridescent light of the moon, Kale saw Abner's iron arrow flit to its target and strike Hermes Wheems' chest with a loud thump.

Wheems pulled out the arrow and carefully laid it down in the bottom of the boat. Then, and in the slowest motion, he reached out for something and pitched it into the Evenlode.

"Murderer," Tori yelled at Abner, and with eyes made wild from the effect of the elixir, she leaped into the roiling, rain-swollen river.

Not stopping to remove his shoes, Kale dove at a run and immediately encountered an onrushing tree stump. He extricated himself from the grasping roots and called her name, but heard nothing over the roar of the black water. "Tor-eeeee!"

The water looked dark as pine pitch. Twice more he was struck by flotsam. He gave up yelling and concentrated on saving his hide. A half-mile downstream, sputtering and coughing, he scrambled up the opposite bank and looked about frantically. Where had she gone? He burst into the alders yelling her name. A few minutes later, cut, bruised, and completely exhausted, he sank to his knees and cried her name, over and over.

As if fueled by his despair the storm returned in full force, dumping sheets of rain against him. From bad to worse, lightning flashed in staccato bursts. Kale hunkered close to the muddy ground, enduring the stinging rain and not caring.

The storm threw sparks from the sky like an iron wheel. Kale slowly raised his head and saw something familiar flit through the alders—Tori's wimple hat.

"Wait! Wait for me!" Blinded by branches, tripping over downed tree limbs, he chased her along the riverbank unable to close the distance. Angry, exhausted, he staggered on until something caught his foot and sent him tumbling down onto the muddy embankment. Only a quick grab at a root kept him from landing in the river.

He stayed there crushed and beaten as a fresh spate of wind thrashed alder branches into a whirlwind of movement. Everything had movement except what lay in the mud at his side. "Oh God, please, not this—no-o-o, not Tori!"

She lay on her back, half in, half out of the river, the rain making strange popping noises on her lifeless, staring eyes.

Kale's stomach leaped into his throat. Fighting back nausea he dragged her up the bank and concentrated on a long-ago, barely remembered CPR class. "Got to get the water out." He undertook the task with the vigor of a Turkish weight lifter. He held her upside down and shook her until his arms gave out, then he squatted down beside her and began the kiss of life.

Ten breaths later Tori let out a huge cough and pushed Kale backward into the mud. He stared at the beauty of her living, breathing, her hair streaming long and wet down her back.

She wasn't wearing the wimple.

"Kale, what happened to me? I had the strangest dream."

"If it had anything to do with Mary Gant, it probably wasn't a dream. Where's your hat? That wimple thing?"

"I threw it away when I fell into the river channel, remember? I'm soaked, Kale. I'm freezing."

Kale pulled her against the warmth of his body. "What possessed you to jump into the river?"

"Poor Wheems, even shot through with an arrow he wanted more elixir. He wanted my half-finished bottle. But when I handed it to him, he fell in the water. I thought to save him. The cold water has rather wakened me to reality, though."

Kale swept wet hair from her face. The elixir had her as half-crazed as Wheems. "Calm down a bit, Tori.

You've suffered a trauma. We need to get you out of this rain."

"Trauma? What are you talking about? I'm just woozy." She pulled away and wobbled off toward the manor.

"Wait! We don't know where Abner is. It could be dangerous." Exhausted, Kale staggered around to where he had last seen the apparition of Mary Gant. "Thank you," he said, and without thinking further of the implications, he slogged away after his partner. He caught up to her beside Harry's half-finished barn and threw her into the shrubbery. Mud oozed into his shoes, and he realized the Evenlode was running willy-nilly over its banks and getting deeper. Something moved in the trees behind the manor. It moved again, and he saw the white hair and rifle. "Abner!" Kale exclaimed and considered his next move carefully and decided Abner was too English to shoot an unarmed man.

"Stay low and well behind me, Tori." He ran in long loping bounds and had almost reached the front door when a bullet cut the air like a zipper. "Maybe he's not English after all," Kale said, his heart pounding like trip hammer.

Tori twirled around like a child on the beach. "Rain hornets!" she yelled, laughing. "Can you hear them? Hey, there's another one." She turned to follow the strange zipping sounds.

The elixir was still on the job. Once again he summoned the strength of a Turkish weight lifter. Running low, he splashed through the deepening water, heaved her onto his shoulder and dashed the stretch between barn footings and the manor house.

Out of breath, exhausted, hardly able to stand, he pressed Tori onto the cold ground and gasped for air while she prattled on about rain hornets.

A bullet ricocheted off the wall, missing his head by inches. He hunkered down beside Tori, put a finger to his lips and whispered, "Quiet now." He crawled toward the front door. At the end of the stone wall, he scooped Tori into his arms and galloped for the front door, bashing it open with his foot.

Bertie stood in the middle of the great room staring into a warm and welcoming fire he'd obviously lit on his own behalf. Startled by Kale's exuberant arrival he turned and said, "I say, old chap. What's happened?"

Kale carried Tori's shivering body toward the warmth of the fire. "A bit of trouble."

"Bloody bad, what? Let me get her a hot toddy. Some dry clothes too, I think."

Kale shook his head. "She's had enough liquor. Make it hot tea. And call Scotland Yard. Abner Snow is out there firing a gun."

Bertie went off in a rush as Kale lay Tori on the rug in front of the fireplace. Firelight danced on her pale skin. He relished the thought of staring at her for hours, drinking in the sight of her, but he came to his senses and pulled a blanket from the settee. He tucked it around her and swept the wet hair from her face. She gazed at him with an unsettling grin, knowing the effect she had upon him.

He couldn't hide his feelings anymore, he knew. It

was useless. She could see it in every fiber of his being as he looked at her. "You frightened me to death out there, Tori. I don't know what I would have done if you'd drowned."

Tori's eyes twinkled in the firelight.

Master Roche's words to Mary Catherine Gant came to mind. "You know, your eyes sparkle like the midnight sky."

She reached up and stroked his face.

"I need you. I love you. I want you forever, Tori. Say you'll marry me."

She only hesitated long enough to make his heart come close to bursting. "Of course I will, Kale. I've wondered for ages what it was going to take to make you ask. I didn't know it was going to take Abner Snow and Hermes Wheems to get you to it."

Kale didn't trust himself to speak. He couldn't believe she'd said yes. His eyes watered as he bent and kissed her, long and sweet.

Afterward, coyness gleamed in her eyes. "We still need a diamond for my finger."

Those that eat hay shall find it, Mary had written. He thought of the horse head flying past and remembered the strange notion it had stirred in him. *Horse buns!* "Maybe," he whispered. He scrambled to his feet and rushed out the door headed for the armory. In there he found the headless horse lying on its side. He ran his hand down the side of the animal. Reaching its hindquarters, he grimaced and stuck his hand into the buttocks. After some clawing about in old excelsior he drew out the largest diamond he'd ever seen.

As he stepped back into the great room he held the diamond between two fingers, the facets gleamed in the firelight. With his gaze playing between Tori and the diamond, he asked, "Will this one do?"

Tori held the jewel between her thumb and forefinger, and grinned from ear to pretty ear. They both looked at it slightly dazed, but it remained there flickering in the firelight.

Bertie returned, clothes and tea in hand, with the rest of the gang in tow.

"Tori, you're all right," Neddy exclaimed. "We thought Wheems had done you in."

Tori pulled the blanket closer and sat up. "All Wheems wanted was the elixir. The poor dear was addicted to the stuff. He knew Abner was after it, and he had to get to it first. He thought we were going to steal it, like we did the brandy at the hotel. His life must have been one long hallucination."

Neddy bent down and felt her forehead. "You're lucky you survived that swim."

"All I remember is a dream. I dreamed of Mary Gant."

Kale smiled, but said nothing.

"Well, all's well that ends well. I called the police. Abner is still lurking about in the woods, but they'll flush him out, and he'll be carted off for the murder of Wheems."

"Never," said Harry. "They'll need a body. I doubt the Evenlode will give them one." He leaned against the huge stones of the fireplace. "I think Wheems was just a dupe. He was into Mary Gant's elixir and made the mistake of sharing it with his only friend, Potter, the gardener. And Potter made a deal with that mining engineer Cassidy to find the source. They were probably going to double-cross Wheems and split it. When Cassidy disappeared, Potter must have thought he'd been double-crossed. But then, Cassidy's body turned up, and the game was on again."

"Cassidy's death was Lord Caddington's doing."

"Lord who?"

Kale cleared his throat. He gave them an abbreviated version of Catherine's story. "Unfortunately, the trap that caught Cassidy went off a few hundred years too late."

"How do you know all that?" asked Harry.

Kale grinned. "That's why I'm the publisher and you're the detective."

"None of that matters," Neddy said. "The elixir in the cellar will be more than enough to pay the back taxes. Galley Press will rise again."

Kale shook his head. "We can't sell that stuff. It's too addictive. It's taken too many lives."

"Exactly why we'll hand it over to the government as payment on the back taxes and let them worry what to do with it," Harry concluded.

Tori grinned. "And we do have the diamond."

"But we still don't know what happened to Mary," Kale said.

Tori sighed. "I think Granny is right. Based on what you read in Catherine's diary, I think she really did go off to America."

"What about Potter the gardener, and John Edwards, the barman?" Neddy asked.

"Abner Snow didn't kill them, if that's what you're thinking. He's the one that torched Galley Press to get the recipe, though. The monks hired him, thinking he'd do the job, return the recipe quietly, and stay mum for the right sum of green. But Abner got the scoop on the goods from Wheems and Potter, and decided there was more to be had than money for returning a recipe."

"So Potter really did fall out the window?"

"I suspect so. The stone that Potter was crowned with, the one the chief inspector was so concerned about, came from Wheems' tunnel. Potter used it on your head. Then his jump from Tori's window went funny and he whacked his own noggin."

"And that barman, John Edwards?"

"He probably sampled the spirits he stole from that fine food shop in Oddington, got drunk, and fell into that river."

Tori cleared her throat and held the diamond up to the firelight. "Well, I'm glad to know all those murders were about the elixir and not this beautiful diamond. I'd hate to have it tarnished with such as that."

She looked at the thoughtful faces around her. "Why so glum? The mystery is solved. My dear Mary Gant was indeed upstanding after all, turning over the recipe and the goods even if things did go a bit awry. And we're all back in business again. I have a book to write."

Neddie nodded. "Bertie has put Wychwood on the map, for sure, with the press we'll get over all this. And the town will be thriving inside a year, don't you think? Harry, you need to quit investing in horses and start looking into some of that village real estate. With a bit of smart business tactics, there's going to be a housing boom around here. Just watch and see. We'll buy up some of the old houses, put in sewers and water, and make this the newest prime spot to live. We'll be rich."

Flabbergasted, Kale glanced from the diamond to Harry, then to Bertie, Neddy, and finally settled on Tori, still wrapped in a blanket and soggy, yet still confident and serene. Her dark hair fell down her back, thick and full, her eyes dancing with happiness. Kale could see that special look, her softness, her playful laughter—she was the real treasure.